The Low Voices

MANUEL RIVAS The Low Voices

Translated from the Galician
by Jonathan Dunne

Harvill *Secker*
LONDON

10 9 8 7 6 5 4 3 2 1

Harvill Secker, an imprint of Vintage,
20 Vauxhall Bridge Road,
London SW1V 2SA

Harvill Secker is part of the Penguin Random House group of companies whose addresses can be
found at global.penguinrandomhouse.com

Penguin
Random House
UK

First published with the title *As voces baixas* in Galicia by Edicións Xerais de Galicia in 2012

A CIP catalogue record for this book is available from the British Library

ISBN 9781846558672

This book has been selected to receive financial assistance from English PEN's 'PEN Translates!'
programme, supported by Arts Council England. English PEN exists to promote literature and our
understanding of it, to uphold writers' freedoms around the world, to campaign against the
persecution and imprisonment of writers for stating their views, and to promote the friendly
cooperation of writers and the free exchange of ideas. www.englishpen.org

Published with the support of the Creative Europe programme of the European Union

The European Commission support for the production of this publication does not constitute an
endorsement of the contents which reflects the views only of the authors, and the Commission
cannot be held responsible for any use which may be made of the information contained therein

Typeset by Palimpsest Book Production Limited, Falkirk, Stirlingshire
Printed and bound in Great Britain by Clays Ltd, St Ives PLC

There are short quotations in this book from the following publications: Juan Rulfo, *Pedro
Páramo*, translated by Margaret Sayers Peden (Grove Press, 1994); Rosalía de Castro, *Galician
Songs*, translated by Erín Moure (Small Stations Press-Xunta de Galicia, 2013); André Breton,
What Is Surrealism? Selected Writings, translated by various (Pathfinder Press, 1978); Manuel
Curros Enríquez, 'To Rosalía', translated by Jonathan Dunne: in Xesús Alonso Montero,
Manuel Curros Enríquez e Federico García Lorca cantan en vinte linguas a Rosalía de Castro
(Edicións do Patronato, 1994); Valentín Lamas Carvajal, *The Peasant's Catechism*, translated by
Kirsty Hooper: in Jonathan Dunne (ed.), *Anthology of Galician Literature 1196–1981* (Edicións
Xerais de Galicia-Editorial Galaxia-Xunta de Galicia, 2010); Ramón del Valle-Inclán, *Lights of
Bohemia*, translated by John Lyon (Aris & Phillips, 1993); César Vallejo, *The Complete
Posthumous Poetry*, translated by Clayton Eshleman and José Rubia Barcia (University
of California Press, 1978).

Penguin Random House is committed to a sustainable future for our business, our readers
and our planet. This book is made from Forest Stewardship Council® certified paper.

To Xesús González Gómez, author of *The Secret Language*, who one day, in the Raval in Barcelona, talked to me about the 'low voices'.

1

First Fear

We were alone, María and I, hugging in the bathroom. Fugitives from terror, we hid in the dark chamber. On stormy days, you could hear the sea's roar. Today it was the rusty, asthmatic mutter of the cistern. Finally, we heard her voice. Calling for us. With unease, to begin with. Then with growing anxiety. We had to respond. Show signs of life. But she took the initiative. We heard her panting, hurried footsteps, the eager sniffing of someone picking up a scent. María drew back the bolt. My mother pushed open the door, bringing the light with her, a storm still in her eyes. Her fear was that of someone who comes home and finds no trace of the children she left playing calmly. Our fear was more primitive than that. It was our first fear.

My mother, Carme, worked as a milkmaid. We rented the ground floor of a house on Marola Street, in the district of Monte Alto in A Coruña. My father had recently returned from South America, from La Guaira, where he'd worked in construction, scaling the summits of buildings and climbing the sky on fragile scaffolding. A quick emigration, just enough time to save the money to buy a plot of land. Many years later, in his old age, he confessed a weakness, he who wasn't in the habit of opening up

The author and his sister María

his secret zone: he suffered from vertigo. All his life, he'd had vertigo. And a large part of that life had been spent on building sites, as a bricklayer's mate and finally as a master builder. Never, until he retired, did he confide in anyone. About his vertigo. About the fact he felt horror inside when he was down on the ground, looking up, and above all when he was up in the air, looking down. Panic from the very first step. But his foot always went in search of the second step. And the second step always led to the third.

'Why didn't you say?'

'What would happen to a workman who went around saying he suffered from vertigo? Who would take him on? *Vertigo?* The word didn't even exist!'

He almost died in La Guaira, stuck in a hut on the hillside, between the forest and a few other shacks, but only he knew about this. During his fever, his sole connection with reality was the voice of a parrot that kept intoning a woman's name: 'Margarita! Margarita!' He knew it existed, this bird. Perhaps the woman as well. One day, he thought he heard, 'Go cry in the valley, old parrot!' But he never saw them, the bird or the woman. When he got better, one Sunday, on his day off from work, he went looking for the parrot. He wanted to talk to it, to offer it his thanks. It had been his only thread to life. But he never found it. My father didn't give this story a magical interpretation. In that place, birds, like people, came and went.

Early in the morning, he would drink a black coffee and leave on his Montesa. Our father, who had returned. Before that, he had a Vespa – and then a Lambretta, which formed part of our family's mythology since it could carry us all without a whimper, with that sense of self-denial displayed by certain domestic appliances. That was his breakfast: black coffee, piping hot. Whenever he had a cold or the flu, he would double the dose of coffee and take an aspirin. He had an almost fanatical faith in acetylsalicylic acid. When his body turned against him and one leg refused to walk, he had to be admitted to hospital. The doctors who operated on his leg found traces of at least two heart attacks. He'd survived these attacks in secret, but silences like that usually write in Braille on a tunnel of the body. Only once, in passing, did he remark that he'd lost the strength in his arms. Whenever he lifted them to operate on a ceiling, they would put up a heavy resistance. He would look at them in surprise, as at two old, unruly companions. Of the memories that used to make him laugh, one was of his youth as a musician in various dance orchestras and of the drummer so taken up with the others' playing that he missed his cue. The paso doble ground to a halt, suspended somewhere in the night, until the conductor's apocalyptic command made itself heard: 'Cymbals, boy! Let the wonders of the world ignite!' An order issued in this way, like a cosmic outburst, sounded like part of the spectacle, but it still took the boy a little time to re-establish the connection. Wonders. Cymbals. The paso doble. Him. In the end, the drummer got going and made the whole night tremble. So, whenever my father's arms grew tired on site, whenever he noticed a lack of energy, he didn't think about a possible heart attack, but about the infallible outburst 'Cymbals, boy! Let the wonders of the world ignite!'

Just as my father couldn't possibly suffer from vertigo, so my mother couldn't possibly fall ill. There were only two moments of real peace. One was on her way to church on a Sunday morning. Not the Mass itself so much as going to Mass. That opiate journey, that *translation*. The other moment was when she had the opportunity to read. Her turn with the newspaper. Having cooked a meal, cleaned, washed, scrubbed, put everything in order, she had this means of escape. A few minutes of total abstraction. The same with books, any book that happened

4

to be lying about the house. This relationship, this happiness, was admirable. You could shout there was a fire, a flood, anything. Our mother would remain entranced. Trapped. Abducted. She wouldn't reply. Wouldn't even look up. Her only reaction was to draw closer to the object of vigil.

There were times when it seemed it would pass, this business of falling ill. 'I don't feel so well, I'm going to lie down for a while.' And the time of healing would last as long as a Mass or a reading. When the disease finally arrived, it wasn't in the manner of the story she used to tell us. It didn't come on a visit.

'Who is it?' asks the old peasant farmer in bed, surprised by a knock one winter's night.

'It's me!' says an unmistakable voice. 'Open up at once!'

This goes on until the old farmer plucks up the courage to say, 'Off with you! There's no one at home.'

And Death mutters, 'It's just as well I didn't come, then.'

That's where I should start. With the murmuring of the first laughter associated with one of her many stories. For instance, a sailor who has survived a shipwreck is captured by a tribe of cannibals. They start cooking him in a pot and add lesser ingredients, tubers and pulses, on the side. As the water heats up and the anthropophagites dance around the fire, building up an appetite, the Galician dives down into his own stew and tucks into potatoes and peas. The head cannibal cries out in admiration, 'Look how happy our food is!' This way of saying goodbye was a form of heroism that filled us with pride. Our hero got eaten by cannibals, yes, but it was an optimistic story. Like the stories by Carlos O'Xestal we used to listen to on the radio, on a Sunday lunchtime. A bagpiper and storyteller, O'Xestal was a strange celebrity during our childhood. His heroes were common people, the humblest there were, who triumphed by means of ingenuity and irony. And who spoke Galician, something that was very unusual on radio broadcasts. The biggest laughs O'Xestal got were when he mimicked those trying to disguise their accent, like covering up a blemish, in such comical situations as that of the young man who missed the ship sailing from A Coruña to Buenos Aires, and when he got back home, having never left Galicia, did so talking like a writer of tangos. The Galician language belonged to this world, but there was a problem with it. Places, moments and situations in which it sounded like a sin on the lips. It lived in the caverns of mouths, but somehow eccentrically, like a tramp that studies the path and company before starting to walk. Once an acquaintance of my parents visited them to let them know he'd finally been accepted as a janitor at some bank. They congratulated him. My father remarked, 'You'll have to buy yourself a new suit . . .' He replied, with a curious exposition of textile sociolinguistics, 'It's bought already! Yesterday, I tried it on with a tie. As soon as I tightened the knot, I broke into magnificent Spanish!'

O'Xestal made almost everybody laugh by laughing at almost everybody, with goads that sometimes pricked the sensitive skin of taboos and complexes. From time to time, he would perform at banquets, in front of the highest authorities on a visit to Galicia. The occasional permissiveness that is granted to the buffoon or comic. Until he suddenly disappeared. The voice on the radio. The pictures, always in traditional clothes, in the papers. O'Xestal's disappearance wasn't something I was aware of at the time. The truth is I'd lost interest in that kind of autochthonous humour. My mind had moved on to other things. Until one day, I came across a news item in which the humorist made his reappearance – but not in the entertainment section, in the section about accident and crime. A police report that talked about a raid in which various people considered a 'social menace' had been detained. Among them was O'Xestal. I interviewed him years later. I was appalled by his account. The abuse, the humiliation, the terrible experience of prison in Badajoz. All for the 'crime' of being homosexual. During the Franco years, the law lumped 'pimps, villains and homosexuals' into one group. By the time he left prison, marked as an outlaw, he was a rebel. A revolutionary. Leading a modest life with his mother in a small village on the coast (Lema, in Baldaio), he risked his neck at the front of a resistance movement to prevent the appropriation of a large nature reserve. Interwoven with his biography, his old stories acquired a different meaning. There was plenty of pain behind the humour. I thought about him not long ago – his ironic smile that never says goodbye, that permeates wakes, that tries to cross over into the beyond – when I saw a slogan painted in tar along the wall of a coastal cemetery, which said of the dead, 'You poachers!'

Or perhaps it was a message from the dead for the living . . .

There is a conversation I shall never forget. An immaterial 'property' from the Department of Unauthorised Childhood Recordings. One of those times in the book of life when the mouth of literature spontaneously makes itself known. We are already living in Castro de Elviña. The winter has come wading into Galicia. Fierce, sullen and cold. An unending downpour. Days of no work, the wind howling around the gaps in buildings. My father has been restless, cornered, for several days, the condensation on the window framing the tenth legion of storm clouds.

Suddenly he bursts out:

'I wish I could have a week in prison!'

My mother is knitting. A new creature is coming. Is on the way. She's been knitting tiny articles of clothing for days, weeks, as her belly keeps growing.

'I wish I could have seven days in hospital!'

María and I are doing our homework at the kitchen table.

We glance at each other. Prison? Hospital? The future looks promising. They have a communication code we have yet to fathom. It seems my mother's response was convincing. They smile. Half smile. Weave a rumour. The warp of a murmur. Fall quiet. They are the existentialist avant-garde. They are exhausted. They have extracted words from the grottoes of their gums.

He didn't talk much, and was never rhetorical, even though he'd give off sudden sparks, as when he remembered the odd excessive binge: 'We drank like Cossacks!' The way he said it, I felt comfortable as the son of a Cossack. The pronunciation of the exoticism 'Cossacks', his eyes opening wide in amazement, reflected the historical nature of the deviation. He also used to say, 'That is worth a *potosí*!' What was a *potosí*? A *potosí* was a *potosí*. A mysterious measure of wealth I handled thanks to my father. And when Potosí appeared on a map in the school encyclopaedia as the name of some silver mines in Bolivia, it was already part of our family heritage. I was drawn in as well by the expression he used to define maximum ignorance: 'He's such a brute he doesn't even know the names of trees.' In the *Odyssey*, Odysseus only manages to convince the blind, incredulous Laertes that he is really his son when he recalls the name and number of the trees, as his father taught him, in the orchard on Ithaca, which would one day be his. When she evoked this passage in class, our teacher's voice would break and, with a bit of imagination, you could see the orchard in her oceanic eyes. We knew that Luz Pozo was also a poet and pianist. A mature woman the whole school was in love with, from the youngest student to the military veteran who took gym, passing through the caretaker, the French *lectrice* and all the teachers of religion. If anyone wasn't in love with her, it was through the misfortune of not having met her. We had heard about poets who crossed Galicia diagonally on motorbikes at weekends, hundreds of miles, just to see her. And we knew it was true when, years later, she left on a motorbike with the poet Eduardo Moreiras. But now we're in her class at school. Luz enters the classroom, followed by an erotic wake whose special quality is to promote greater peace than excitement. Eros, taken by the hand, alights on the study material, the challenge of forcing open Luis de Góngora's 'Polyphemus'. But it's one thing to talk about literature, it's another thing entirely to hear the mouth of literature. And that is what I heard, quite clearly, when Luz Pozo read what was happening in the orchard on Ithaca, at that precise moment when memory merged with the manuscript of the earth, Odysseus listing all the fig trees, apple trees, pear trees and vines. There was a second text, a murmur only I could hear in my father's mouth when he wished to signal an extreme case of ignorance: not knowing, not wanting to know, the names of the trees that surround you.

Whenever he argued with my mother, he would use an expression I found cryptic, with a hidden meaning:

'You are the Spirit of Contradiction.'

She never held back what she was thinking. She was sweet, but not docile. At that time, the laws regarding women were even more shocking than people's attitudes towards them. A woman was a subordinate being. She could do nothing without her husband's approval. But my mother could not accept such a submissive role, and my father knew it. So, whenever he felt thwarted, he would allude to the influence on my mother of that invisible creature, the Spirit of Contradiction, which soon formed part of our domestic mythology. In their own way, neither of them was particularly sociable. They constituted a pair of conjugal recluses, but their solitudes were different. My father avoided crowds whenever he could. When it came to sporting events, he experienced real aversion. He tried, unsuccessfully, to engender in me the same hatred he felt towards football. After that, he tried to keep me away from the grounds. We had a neighbour, Gregorio, a technician for Radio Coruña, who offered to take me along to Riazor Stadium. For my father, those epic hours when Deportivo was playing out its very existence, which was every Sunday afternoon, were a good time for us to go out in the garden. I felt miserable, and he would try to persuade me that paying to see two factions of adult men chasing after a ball, driven on by a roaring mob, represented a kind of defeat for humanity. Until he admitted his own defeat and I was allowed to go with Gregorio to Riazor. After leaving the stadium, we would drop by the house of some relatives. Their building was connected to a large hairdressing salon. As the adults talked, I would peer into that enchanted world, with its mirrored walls and the chairs with disturbing helmets in which heads would undergo a metamorphosis (that enigmatic expression, 'to have a perm'!), a scene that is now deserted, but alert, with the futuristic nostalgia of murmurs, colours and aromas. The enamel of dragonflies flashing on absent nails. There was a charm about the place one resisted as much as one was drawn to it. The charm of what it would be like to be a woman. Or what one would be like as a woman. Back at home, after night had fallen, my parents were listening to the radio. They used to do this with the light out, the only illumination coming from the radio dial. Our house hanging on the hillside looked just like a ship. The wind whistling over the harmonica of the roof, the beams from the lighthouse licking our darkness. Special effects from outside that heightened the suggestiveness of the radio. We were both in and out. The voices and static formed part of nature. Life had a storytelling vocation. I had been at Riazor, that other bustling, suspended spaceship, amid the ebb and flow of roars. I had been in the fantastic hair salon, in that shadowy light of large chrysalises. And now, leaning on the window of night, I felt like an equal next to the Man Who Despises Football and the Woman Who Talks To Herself.

They could both be very silent or very talkative. I learned that language had seasons. Days when words sprouted, days when mouths rested, days when they talked to themselves, days when dry leaves fell from lips and went spinning off towards a bitter destination. There was a special characteristic about my father's speech that made it different from that of most adult males. He never swore or cursed, even when he was expressing extreme annoyance. He never called on God, the Virgin, the saints of the Church or the angels in heaven. He never even bothered the devil. That seemed natural enough in a believer like my mother, but it surprised me in a man who never set foot inside a church. In fact, men at Mass on a Sunday were a rarity. They would attend burials, funerals and anniversaries. Also High Mass on a feast day. But even on those occasions most would remain outside, in the yard, and those who went inside would take up position at the back of the building. Men didn't kneel. They remained standing in that area of half-light under the choir loft. It was also strange for a man to receive communion. To participate in communion, to receive the sacred form, required confession. And that – going to confess to the priest – was something that tried my father's patience. Whenever they argued about this, it would have been normal to expect a stream of curses.

The author's parents at their wedding

'What is the priest? He's . . .'

Airily, he answered his own question with the most outrageous euphemism he could find:

'A man! He's nothing more than . . . a man.'

But that came later, long after our first fear. Memory goes a-wandering, it crosses fields, darts across the Avenue, walks like Charlie Chaplin the Tramp inside the Hercules Cinema. Or walks like women with things on top of their heads. All of them – well, almost all – carried something. A prolongation of basic things. Take, for example, the walk of the milkmaid. My mother would begin by delivering to Monelos. Then she'd get on the trolleybus and start again on San Xoán Street, at Asunción's shop. One of the places she served was a military establishment attached to the cavalry. One day, a soldier whispered to her, 'You can put water in the milk, don't worry, they add even more once it's here.' Meanwhile, we were living on Marola Street, renting the ground floor. María can't have been three and I was under two. Back then, before it was blocked by the violent actions of the land registry, the street had an open horizon and ran into the surroundings of the Tower of Hercules. Very near our home was a place known as the Farmhouse. No, it wasn't an ethnographic museum. It was a real farmhouse at the limits of the city with the sea. A house with cows and a traditional cart. That was a real journey into space, going on that cart. The fields that bordered the provincial prison were fertile ground with lush crops and potatoes that tasted of the sea. There were meadows, willows, a choir of blackbirds in the field next to Lapas Beach. The cows moved between the city limits and the cliffs. In my memory, they represent a canvas of mythological pop art. How the Tower of Hercules, declared a world heritage site, could benefit from a few amphibian cows in the sun! That space is now occupied by fixed sculptures and a municipal obsession with lawns, the green acrylic laminating the sylvan colours. The cows of time have disappeared. They're mooing out at sea.

We were alone on that ground floor on Marola Street. We were sitting on the floor. I was playing with a toy lorry. There was a loose tile, which could be removed. Underneath it, a bug, a cockroach. I was trying to grab it, with good intentions, I wanted to give it a ride on the lorry, but it kept running away, anticipating my hand's movement. And then María lifted her head, all alert, all of her smiling. She jumped to her feet and ran towards the window that looked onto the street. I followed her, as always. In symmetry. She walked with her feet pointing outwards, bandy-legged, and I was pigeon-toed, with my feet pointing inwards. Each of us walked as best he could. Aunt Paquita had a limp. She would exclaim joyfully, 'The lame one's here!' And there'd be murmuring: 'How pretty you look! How well you limp, Paquita!' But now we were alone. María ran with her feet pointing outwards and I ran with my feet pointing inwards. We heard music in the street. Saw clowns throwing streamers. Fireworks. A party. The window was a marvellous screen. Until suddenly two monsters appeared, filling it completely, with heartless eyes, their noses banging against the glass. We'd never seen danger up so close before. The horror.

'You fools!' said our mother. 'It was only two carnival giants. Isabella and Ferdinand, the Catholic Monarchs.'

14

2

Sitting on the Emigrant's Suitcase

For a year, my seat at the strange nursery was a suitcase. I felt as if I were sitting inside the ferry terminal or in customs.

After our first fear, the attack of the giants, our mother decided my sister María and I shouldn't spend so much time on our own while she did her rounds as a milkmaid. Sometimes my godmother, Amelia, would look after us. My godfather, Pepe Couceiro, was a fan of mechanics and scientific progress. For a time, he focused all his ingenuity on combustion engines. He could build a two-seater car out of a motorbike. His intention was to travel the Galician roads inside that capsule and even go beyond the Pyrenees, to Europe. He had an enigmatic expression: in advanced countries, 'all the countryside is landscape'. And he would gaze at the horizon nearby with scientific fatalism, sorry that not even an inch of Galicia would ever be redeemed. He had a spirit like Marco Polo's. So much so that he ended up working as a seller of spices, an expert in that precious, aromatic merchandise. The first time I had the impression someone was formulating a revolutionary thought, toppling the universal system of weights and measures, was when my godfather revealed a little pigment on the end of his forefinger, stared at me and solemnly declared, 'A kilo of saffron is worth more than a kilo of gold!'

One day, he took me on one of his expeditions as a spice merchant. I remember it as the first real journey of my life.

'To the end of the world!' he exclaimed enthusiastically.

I had a certain tendency to take things literally. I was prepared to go to the end of the world, but was also a little worried. Until he patted me on the head: 'You'll see. We'll get to Finisterre!' And we did. The journey lasted all day, like the sun, from dawn to dusk. Along the Costa da Morte, or Death Coast, towards the outer reaches. The two of us stuck in the capsule of a small car, on this occasion a SEAT 600. As we stopped off at shops, grocers and restaurants, my godfather, quite a short man, grew for me in historic stature. I felt proud to be accompanying the spice trader. Paprika, cinnamon, saffron! We were very well received, heralds of plenty, bearers of precious merchandise: tiny envelopes containing fragments of colours, aromas, tastes, which would scatter when they were opened. Or tins of pepper, illustrated with prints of exotic women that accorded with the nature of the treasure. I'd seen women – my own mother, neighbours – filling these envelopes and folding them in a flash, with dazzling speed, and at that precise moment the women looked like the beauties in the prints because they accompanied their labour, the swiftness of their fingers, with the lightness of jokes and laughter. I'd noticed a difference between women and men when they were working in a group. Men were much more taciturn.

On the way back, in the town of Carballo, my godfather announced, 'Now we're going to buy a *souvenir*!' What was this *souvenir*? And he added with happy determination, 'So you can take it to your mother.' When someone said 'to your mother', it almost always meant a present for the whole house, for everybody. We learned this quickly enough. And what he bought was a large loaf of bread the child in question couldn't get his arms around. A soft, hemispherical loaf that on the journey home seemed to ferment on the lap of the sleeping child's body.

'What bread! It's like another world!'

It was bread, yes. But it was also something other than bread. What a shame! I'd forgotten the word. *Souvenir*. My first *souvenir*.

There was other secret knowledge. The initiatory ground, the first nation, had the form of a triangle, if we consider three monumental markers as vertices. The first was the seaside cemetery of Santo Amaro. Regarding this place, I remember a neighbour, in conversation with my father, praising the cemetery in the highest possible terms: 'This cemetery is the healthiest in the world!' And he explained its qualities: well oriented, luminous and breezy. The second vertex, very close to our home on Marola Street, was the provincial prison. Not so healthy. Back then, at dusk, from up on the cliffs, one could see the prisoners in the courtyard. From time to time, there would be a snatch of song. It was a windy place, next to the sea, which was almost always rough. In fact, the wind and the beating of the waves integrated every murmur, shout or voice into a stubborn, musical warp. The only thing that escaped was the intermittent sound of a stonemason who had his workshop in a hut. The mallet beating the chisel he used to sculpt granite, crosses, gravestones, dominated with its handmade time like a bitter clock. When the stonemason finished for the day, silence would fall to its knees, as if this was what the chisel had been working on. Some days, relatives would clamber up the cliffs and communicate with the prisoners using coloured handkerchiefs in a code of signals. 'Look, there he is, so near!' So far. From that unsettling lookout, everything seemed at hand and inaccessible. A greeting at a distance of several yards, but years away. It was necessary to find hope. To turn around. To search for the third vertex. And there it was!

The lighthouse.

It was the light of a living creature. A light that awoke, lived at night and slumbered at daybreak. When there was a thick fog, it was this same creature that mooed like a cow. It wasn't a sudden, blinding glare. It gradually stretched, fed its flashes with the last embers of dusk, at that hour when everything becomes a stranger to itself. The Tower of Hercules gave off light, and at the same time you had the sensation it was gathering the dark side of everything it licked. Of what was happening on the cliffs, in crevices, on corners. 'What corner will we see each other on, Monte Alto?' Monte Alto was a district full of corners where many names of bars, shops, workshops evoked the corners of the map of America. It was easy in that place to go from Montevideo to Buenos Aires. The light of the lighthouse licked and gathered everything. Shadows, dreams, secrets. It may still have them. Under the lighthouse, in an ossuary of light. The flashes, luminous blades, ran over the tiles, filtered through the slats in the blinds, momentary bursts that scythed the rooftops but left the darkness even darker than before. The lantern of the lighthouse sewed what was outside onto what was inside: wakefulness and sleep. The unending sea and the walls of narrow rooms.

But now we're on our way to the first school. The strange nursery.

We weren't old enough to go to school in an official centre, and 'children's gardens' didn't exist then, even as a euphemism. There was no sense of drama the first day. María and I quickly understood that our whole physical and emotional energy should be directed not at the useless effort of resisting, but at the will to clear a way and find somewhere to sit as soon as possible. That first little school, in a private home, was on a parallel street in Monte Alto and was run by two sisters who acted as nursemaids, sentinels and mistresses. It was enough for them to keep track of numbers. The children in that concentration room were like grains of sand. But something extraordinary happened: the expansion of space, one of the least studied features in the history of popular architecture. Marcial Suárez has already said that Allariz is the place in the world with the most churches per square Catholic.

For almost a year in the strange nursery, I sat on a suitcase. I don't know whether it was a question of fate or not, but it really was a suitcase. Not the metaphor of a suitcase. The first day, amid all the uproar, I looked at the suitcase and the suitcase looked at me, the causality that took the form of a woman's divine voice saying, while pushing me with implacable delicacy, 'You, shrimp, sit down on that suitcase.' Before one had learned how to read or write, one already understood the iconography of the suitcase. Almost all houses had one or several of these suitcases. Now that I think about it, the suitcase's measure was just about that of a square child. But I never looked to see what was inside the suitcase in the strange nursery. What I held, and never let go, was a fuchsia, almost fluorescent plastic briefcase. Nobody ever asked me to open it. So one day I did it myself. Pulled on the zip. There was nothing there.

Years later, at school in Castro de Elviña, the teacher asked us one day what we wanted to be when we were older. He didn't follow a pedagogy of participation, so we remained cautiously silent and waited to see what would happen. Where was the question aimed? Why did he want to know what we wanted to be? What was it he really wanted to hear? And then, in that mute silence, like a festive whoop, came the voice of someone we called Red of the Wood, who shouted from the back, 'Emigrants!' The teacher was taken aback and fell into a mournful silence. The external wall had a large lattice window. Whenever a pane fell out or broke, it took a long time to be replaced. So there were always holes out to the open, through which the wind whistled or the rain drove. One might say the holes used these moments of bewilderment to make themselves heard. The teacher seemed to become aware of them, the gaps in the wall, the damp stains, the peering in of the elements. He who had just been talking to us about the time when Spain was a huge empire 'where the sun never set'. How much he – and we – liked that phrase! Solar precision brought history closer. We were in a remote place, in a battered building, the sacks of powdered milk sent by the Americans piled up in a corner, but the sun was there as well, not setting, at least for the moment, and the teacher was kind enough to implicate us all in a great, imperial epic. We had dominated the world. We had carried the cross the world over. We even used to go out collecting money in order to save the souls of Chinese children. But now the teacher had asked what we wanted to be when we were older and this sincere voice, coming from the back of the class, had the effect of a fallen pane that smashes on the ground. The children of the Empire dreamed of becoming emigrants.

That suitcase, the one in the strange nursery, must have had at least enough room for two emigrant children. So one day they sat a classmate down next to me. We never spoke. We never even looked at each other. I just asked for permission to get up and go to the toilet. I went down the corridor on my own. There were framed photographs of women on the walls. Not the teachers. My attention was drawn to the hairstyles, the clothes, the long black gloves of one, another in what looked like a man's suit with a smoking cigarette holder between her fingers. Above all, their look. They were the ones who looked out or stopped looking. I pushed open a door. It happened to be to the kitchen. In the middle, a large table with a green and white checkered tablecloth. On top of the table, like an effigy, sat a cat. An unbelievable cat, unlike all the cats I'd seen up until that moment, with long, immaculate white hair and a glowing aura, a celestial cat with a bow and a little bell around its neck. The cat glanced at me, over its shoulder, with indifference. And it was then I realised that I'd set foot in America.

3

The Clandestine
Children's Staircase

In the strange nursery, sitting on the suitcase one day, I heard María's voice.

It was a voice that came from on high. So I lifted my head and saw her standing on the table, above all the noise, with a spelling book in her hand. It really was my sister. But the voice was new: it had been born that very day. María was a little more than a year older than me. I didn't even have a spelling book. I went to school with an empty briefcase, which I wouldn't let go for anything in the world. And now, there she was. Reading aloud, in the middle of an astonished silence. Without making any mistakes, without stuttering. Reading syllables, whole sentences. She was capable of pronouncing the divine words '*mi mamá me ama, mi mama me mima*'. And '*uvas iglesia bicicleta*'. She turned page after page, and the teacher asked her excitedly to carry on, carry on, wanting to see whether what was happening was really true or just a superstition. I already knew my sister had a special relationship with words. She was a verbivore. She went out gathering words and carried them home. You can tell because of the separation in her teeth, in early photos, that her mouth was full of words. It must have had something to do with our family. My mother was a verbivore as well. She talked to herself in a way that bewitched us, without realising, without even knowing we were listening. In the house or houses we lived in, there were no books at that time. The first poems I heard were in my mother's solitary mouth, poems she recited to herself or to someone who kept her company in her imagination, even when she was washing or scrubbing. Whatever it was, it was something strange, captivating, but also disturbing. It was the mouth of literature, unannounced. This being nourished by the sound of words was a family secret, however. I didn't know María had learned how to read from one day to the next, but nor was I surprised. There were herbivores and carnivores. And then there were those who fed on words. There were plenty of that species in my family. One of the first I discovered was my uncle Francisco, my mother's brother, who was a barber. For us children, a haircut was a kind of torture. Our heads were shaved without further ado. As a precaution against lice, we were given a convict haircut. In nature, it would seem there is a desire for style, which is revealed, for example, in symmetry. In the way a sea urchin grows or the degree at which a fig tree bends on the coast. In the flight of a flock of starlings. Or the monstrous threat posed to predators by the drawings on the wings of certain butterflies. These are observations and enchantments, marks in the history of the look. Detecting humiliation also forms part of the primitive equipment of some species.

It was to see oneself in the mirror and feel humiliated, as when one suffers an inexplicable punishment. The barber's chair, where adults sat so contented and trusting, a magazine or newspaper open in their hands, more or less indifferent to the artistic process being performed on their heads, was an executioner's chair for us little ones. Our locks fell to the floor, the wild beast retreated. The head was humiliated. But that wasn't the feeling with which one left Uncle Francisco's barber's shop. Not for stylistic reasons. He wasn't heterodox when it came to the dominant haircut. The scissors and mowing machine advanced implacably over the skull's lawn. But what happened to one's head in that place was secondary. The important thing was the discourse. Uncle Francisco's incessant stream of thought. In reality, a snip-snap of the scissors on high, preceded by a flourish in the air, was not part of the haircut, but the start of a new paragraph.

When long hair became fashionable, we teenagers gradually abandoned him. In the same building as the barber's shop, he lent out a room for a rock band to practise. Uncle Francisco's monologues, of which he had a different one for each client, alternated with this music that had ushered in a fashion he considered disastrous. But he was a narrator above all else, and this situation enabled him to renew his characters and themes. Unlike the haircut, which

On the right, Uncle Francisco and, sitting down, Aunt Manuela

continued unchanged, the storyteller moved with the times. Irony was his trademark. What kept him on the front line.

'Humour, gentlemen, is the pauper's second sauce.'

'And the first one?'

'Hunger. That's the best sauce for eating.'

Only once, as far as he could tell, did Uncle Francisco shut his mouth in the middle of a story and find himself unable to continue. In the story, there was a moment's terror, when some Falangists broke into the house at night to take away his father, my grandfather from Corpo Santo, with the intention of killing him. At this point, the old man he was shaving, a complete stranger, blurted out:

'I may have been one of them.'

And he added with a certain pride, glancing around:

'I may even have been the driver.'

Uncle Francisco held his nerve. Wiped the cut-throat against the leather. Swept it over the old man's face until removing the last speck of foam. Gave him a few smacks of aftershave. Splish, splash!

'Don't ever come here again.'

'How much do I owe?' said the other in surprise.

'Use it to pay for some Masses. Nothing you do will ever be too much to save your soul.'

Whenever he remembered that day, a shadow fell over his eyes. He explained about the razor, his self-restraint over his instinct, not as something that deserved praise, but as a simple condition, the way a good storyteller should be able to hold his nerve.

A few years later, I again see María on a table, surrounded by people. It's in Leonor's shop and pub, in Castro de Elviña. One summer's afternoon, after lunch. Most of the men are outside, working. The hour and the absence of men allow the women to be inside the shop, in the shade. They're also working. Sewing, embroidering, knitting. And María is standing on top of the table. Reading the newspaper aloud. From time to time, they ask her to repeat something. An incident, perhaps. There is no radio or television. María is reading with the lantern of her green eyes, in the midst of a friendly silence. After a while, they lift her down off the table. Caress her. Give her a banana and some cherries. She shares this first wage. Of cherries.

Corpo Santo tasted of cherries.

This was the place where my maternal grandfather, Manuel, lived. We never knew our maternal grandmother, Xosefa. She died young, because of an illness, and left behind ten children. Two perished during the misery that followed the Spanish Civil War. Before that, during the coup of 1936, a Fascist group arrived in the night and dragged my grandfather outside to 'take him for a walk'. He was Republican. And Christian. He was also secretary of the Farmers' and Stockbreeders' Mutual. The fact he could write must have been his downfall. On one occasion, he refused, as secretary, to draw up and sign a contract for the sale of cattle in bad condition. Another time, he declined to validate a sale that had been agreed late in the night, after a card game. On such occasions, Manuel of Corpo Santo's expression of resistance, his way of saying 'I would prefer not to', was 'Gentlemen, we're out of time!' Whenever he went to the mountain for firewood or animal bedding, he would use the fact he was alone to read or write. He lost all sense of time. And he was lucky that death, in this case, also lost all sense of time. Because he was saved by a miracle. He was saved by the shout of the parish priest, whose conscience had taken him to the scene of the crime on horseback.

So it was that, in Corpo Santo, four boys and four girls were raised by my grandfather. They grew like cherry trees. The orchards in Mariñas Douradas, the name of that region, preserved the memory of the French song 'Time of Cherries'. I associate the happiest days with blackbirds. Sometimes, around the beginning of July, a swarm of us cousins would spend the whole day up in the trees, sharing the treasure with mocking blackbirds. When we were small, we stayed there for long periods. As I would often wake up in one bed, having gone to sleep in another, so, for me as a child, it seemed there was a secret passageway linking the hill with the lighthouse to the staircase in Corpo Santo.

The one who really communicated with a large part of the world was my grandfather. He did this from a table he used as a desk, on the upper floor of the house. It was one of those unpredictable places where the globe alights in order to rest. The globe gives the impression it never stops, it orbits, suspended in space, turning on its axis, but this is very tiring and from time to time it looks for somewhere to set down. When the globe settles on a particular point in the world, something happens. To my mind, it used to alight on that modest desk, where there were piles of postcards and letters from the diaspora. Addresses, stamps, photographic views, where the colours of the Promised Land, primary and intense, fermented. The postcards formed a kind of *mappa mundi*. He was a real writer. As the ancient Greeks used to say, 'an interpreter of interpreters'. He wrote letters to emigrants. The 'widows of the living' would come, and he would write down news items and feelings that crossed the sea, beyond Marola, the islet that gave our street its name, the mark of farewell on the bay's mouth. He had very good handwriting. The letters looked like vegetal landscapes. Over in America, if the reader knew how to read, he would see each word and everything named by it, perhaps even a little more. What hadn't been said.

Apart from the small planetary desk, there was another

extraordinary place in Corpo Santo. A staircase with pine steps and wooden sides. It led from the hard-packed earthen floor downstairs to the wooden floor on the second level, where the bedrooms were and the chests with items of value: deeds, seeds and dowries.

During the day, everybody worked hard. But when the frontier of dusk was passed, a wonderful metamorphosis took place. The silent creatures hung their work up on a hook and were summoned to a second life. Around food, wine and fire, words came, bringing news and stories. Downstairs, opposite the hearth, was the cowshed. The cows poked their heads out of the mangers, three irrepressible forces sucking grass and blowing out clouds of steam. The cows' breath was what covered the valley of Corpo Santo every morning. This factory of mist, so realistic, was like a children's story. The adults had other stories for themselves. Stories about the Holy Company, the souls of nostalgic dead people who hanker after a coffee with a few drops of brandy. Wolf stories, with wolf men and women. Adventure stories, stories of emigration. The stowaway who can't make up his mind to get off the ship and so spends his life going to and fro, a secret man, hidden. Stories of fugitives on the mountain, the Maquis. Of crime and revenge. The man who heads to the *festa*, intending to kill a rival, but when he hears the music, reconsiders and throws the knife away, and when the party is over, the other, the one who was due to die, finds the weapon, the moon glinting on its blade, and takes it up, determined, with a fixed purpose . . . Stories of passionate love. In an enclosed convent, where the nuns make dummies of the infant Jesus to sleep next to on Christmas Eve . . .

That was the point at which we were supposed to visit the fields of sleep. The children, off to bed. We went, groaning or pretending to groan. Because we knew this expulsion was not serious. We would remain, invisible and clandestine, sitting on the top step, under a lamp that transmitted the wind outside, the intensity of the stories, the embers of the fire and our hearts. In that lamp, suspended by a twisted wire, light came and went without doing so completely. It was a place of intermittences that attracted moths. The elders' talk kept step with the fire's humour, and our ears with the lamp upstairs. In the window above the sink, we could see the reflected faces talking in the half-light, as if they belonged to another time that was not the past, but was just that: another time. The words fed on the flames, but there came a moment when they fled from the fire into the dark . . .

There were unforgettable nights. As when a letter was read out from a suitor of my aunt Maruxa, a girl of seismic beauty.

To demonstrate his virility, the suitor had written a letter that was recited many times around the fire in Corpo Santo. It began with a wonderful snippet of information: 'Yesterday, I saw you at the fair and you should know that I didn't talk to you.' The laughter made the flames flicker. Further down the page, the gallant author of the letter proceeded to enumerate his properties in order to impress and captivate the letter's recipient. He recorded in calligraphic acres an unending estate of fields, meadows, hills and plots of land. He then gave details about his livestock: 'You should know that we combine seven cows, x number of pigs and at least a hundred Leghorn chickens.' He then added, quite naturally, 'And a father in disconformable health.'

Aunt Maruxa, who later happily married Xoán Agra, a taxi driver from Sada, opened her arms and lifted them to the sky like two exclamation marks: 'You see! I can't possibly marry this man!' The huddle of people killed themselves laughing. And killed the night with a polyphony of little bells. The fire laughed as well, in sparks and smuts. The scene was reflected and painted a picture on the window above the sink. That planisphere in chiaroscuro was the last image to be retained on the eyelid of sleep. Cradled by the low voices, the clandestine children fell asleep on the staircase in Corpo Santo.

4

The War, the Cow
and the First Plane

There was a rumour doing the rounds. A glaring alarm for any who chose to see it in the oblique shadow of the news' typography.

Both my grandfathers felt the claws of the human hunt that was unleashed with the triumph of the 1936 Fascist coup. One was at death's door; the other spent time as a fugitive in the mountains, with some colleagues.

But all I ever heard from them about the war was a couple of stories where they talked about birds. Two omens linked with nature, from which they knew, with a degree of certainty, what was going to happen before it happened.

At the beginning of that July, Manuel Barrós, my grandfather from Corpo Santo, one day came back home mournful and silent, he who was normally so lively and chatty. He didn't feel like eating. And he didn't regain his spirits until he opened his mouth and explained what had happened. On a cart track, there had been a fight between two hoopoes. Two hoopoes? Oh, come on! It can't have been that serious. The truth is he'd seen lots of fights between animals, the blustering of males, but never felt such horror before. The two hoopoes were pecking each other to death, unyieldingly. My grandfather tried to shoo them away, but they paid no attention to his shouts or threatening stick. Those small birds had turned their whole bodies into weapons. Their whole being into an impulse of death. Manuel of Corpo Santo decided to abandon the place of horror. He interpreted this event as a defeat for the whole of nature. Despite not being at all superstitious, he said, 'Something terrible's going to happen.'

In the other story, the one about my paternal grandfather, the presence of a bird was more phonosymbolic. Early one morning, around that same date, Manuel Rivas, a carpenter from Sigrás, was on his way to work with some colleagues in the back of a lorry. There was a thick fog, so thick it could have been kneaded with fingers, and the lorry penetrated it slowly. After a curve, a priest in a cassock appeared by the side of the road, like a ghost. He was a corpulent man, whose figure was exaggerated by an enormous, black felt hat and an expansive umbrella. The workmen were taken aback at such an early hour and slowly scanned the apparition, which was soon left behind. Until one of them, a young man, imitated the call of a carrion crow from the trailer:

'Caw, caw, caw!'

The joke brought about laughter, but there was still time to hear the thunderous reply:

'Go ahead and laugh! We'll all be laughing around the middle of the month!'

It was the start of July. A good month. The month of St James. The month of *festas*. Having recalled this episode, my grandfather would murmur, like someone who has suddenly and surprisingly deciphered a historical enigma, 'He knew it! That priest knew what was going to happen!' I've always been impressed by the potential of this story, of what occurred that morning in the fog.

Someone in possession of a big secret goes and reveals it because he is annoyed at a childish joke.

Manuel, the one from Sigrás, was affiliated to the trade union. And saying 'trade union' on the coast of A Coruña meant the National Confederation of Labour. He spent some time in prison during the two black years (the *bienio negro*) of the Second Spanish Republic, but the judge himself dropped all the charges. He took part in the long, drawn-out strike to achieve an eight-hour working day. Whenever he referred to this struggle, the briefest of incisions into his silence, a libertarian melancholy would emanate from the depths of his irises.

With regard to language, there was a huge difference between the grandfather who was a farmer and the one who was a carpenter. Manuel of Corpo Santo was talkative; he would quickly make conversation. He talked, with great pleasure, whenever he had company, and he talked when he was alone. He sometimes didn't realise this – the fact he was no longer alone – and carried on talking to himself. I remember walking with him, holding his hand, as he talked to himself with growing energy, with the dynamo of his voice, that current transmitted by the squeeze of his hand, the feeling we were about to take off. Manuel of Sigrás, on the other hand, spoke very little. I spent more time with him. I knew him better. But not because of what he said, because of what he kept quiet. He expressed himself using a Morse code of silences. Castro de Elviña was close to O Martinete. We would occasionally go there, María and I. We were looked after by Aunt Felicitas, my father's youngest sister. And we spent long periods in Aunt Amparo's workshop, where the rhythm of the sewing machines kept time with the emotions of the radio serials. My grandparents' house was near a quarry. The open-air mine had advanced implacably and deposited their house on a kind of tremulous cliff. Before the quarry was shut down, life was regulated by a kind of dynamite clock, the hours marked by explosions. When my grandmother was embroidering, there would be a moment more silent than silence. She would lift her needle, there would be an explosion, the trembling of windows, and, without making a remark, she would go back to the laborious construction of her embroidery. When my grandfather returned from work, he would take me with him to a tavern in A Cabana. He would say hello when we arrived, but then we would sit in a corner, on two benches either side of a table. The most common drink was a bowl of white Ribeiro, but he always drank light red wine in a glass and invited me to have a soft drink: Mirinda, orange flavour. And so we would keep each other company, sip by sip. From time to time, he would roll himself a cigarette. The column of smoke was slower and denser than the Celtas my father smoked. It climbed and formed a thick cloud illuminated by the lamp. The exhalation produced an animated design, a landscape. His hair was already silvery by then and, when he removed his beret, it produced a luminous effect, a kind of phosphorescence. I didn't like berets or white hair or wrinkles. I don't think children in general are attracted by the face of old age. But I liked his head. A lot. In his own way, the silent man also used to talk to himself. In between sips and exhalations, he would ponder something. He seemed on the verge of saying it. He glanced up at the cloud. In the background, the cackle of customers at the bar. At which point he would mutter, 'Boh!'

The qualities that were prized most highly in the art workshops of Flanders were 'a fertile look, a sincere hand'. These two conditions were shared by the farmer, the carpenter and the seamstress. My grandmother from Corpo Santo, Xosefa, died soon after the war, when my mother was still a child. The carpenter and the seamstress had three daughters and a son, my father, who ended up being born in Zamora during a snowstorm, when my grandfather was working on the construction of a hospital. The baby was in luck: the first sound he heard was that of his father building a cradle.

Things got complicated after that. This last delivery brought about a discomfort in the seamstress that bothered her continually. She walked like a cloud. In the shadow of a dream. The worst thing for a working-class family, during the post-war years of hunger, was not to have work or land. It was better during those years to be a farmer. The girls were looked after by their aunts. The three women, all single, had worked as housemaids in A Coruña. They'd managed to put something by, they loved each other, looked out for one another, were very sensitive in their dealings. Far removed from macho rudeness and abuse, they'd turned their home into a real doll's house. This is where Amparo, who would later become a successful fashion designer, grew up. She showed textile subtlety in her speech and behaviour. In her workshop, she treated everybody – adults and children, men and women – as if they were cut from the finest cloth in Galicia. My father's destiny was somewhat different. He himself said he lived like a 'little savage'. He barely attended school. In order for him to eat, they sent him to live with his grandparents, who were farmers, so he could pasture the cows. But he didn't eat much. He spent the day between moos, he used to say. And at night, he mulled over the unending litany of the old people's rosary. This was his work for years. Acting as a butler to cows. Early in the morning, he would sometimes pass in front of the doll's house wrapped in scraps of mist from the river. He went so far as to stroke the doorknocker. But he never knocked. The cows were getting away along the riverbank. Amphibian shapes driving through the reeds and fog.

One day, he heard a deafening roar in the sky. It was a twin-engine aircraft, descending right next to the trees. It looked as if it were about to land on top of them. My father said it was so close he could see the pilot's face. A kind of time in suspense. He looked at the pilot and the pilot looked at him. One of the cows was curious to see the pilot's face as well. My father's head was raised, so the cow did the same. The tip of a horn collided with a dimple in his lower jaw. Leaving a shapely scar.

When he was older, there were women who remarked that a scar like that made a man more interesting. They asked him how he'd made that dimple, which was in the manner of Robert Mitchum. And my father replied, with historical precision, 'It was somewhere between a cow and a plane!'

5

Come Back When
You Step on the Sun

He waves nostalgia away, like a fly from his face. My father says,
I can hear him now, 'You thought you had the animal tied, but
it was the animal who had you tied.'

That business of pasturing the cows was something common
to the childhood of all my parents' generation. Everybody, uncles
and aunts, herded cows and sheep at some time. Unending days,
tied to the animal. It's not a metaphor. The small size of the properties, the concern about crossing boundaries, the fear the animal
might suddenly take off, startled by a sting or a sound or a shadow
in the suspicious world of the mountain. This meant you had to
keep it tethered by a rope. And the rope acted as a bitter restraint
on the person in question. Sunk in thought next to the grazing
cow. My mother found pasturing the cows to be a nightmare.
But especially the terror of having to go with Yellow. All cows
that have recently given birth respond to the calls of their calves.
But Yellow responded to all the calls of all the calves, whether or
not they were her own. And she didn't just respond with a mother's moo, that cry that sends a shiver through the grass and
propels clouds forwards. She started running, dragging the girl

with her, until the girl let go of the rope and the cow went leaping over walls and hedges in search of the call. The next day, my mother would try taking her as far away as possible, leading her down deep tracks to the other side of the mountain. Until she thought she was in another world, in another bell jar, where the noises and sounds of Corpo Santo couldn't reach. But someone once said eloquence is in the ear of the listener. Wherever she went, the cow heard a calf calling to her. Until one day the girl decided she wasn't going to keep the rope holding Yellow taut. What's more, she wasn't even going to look at her. She wished she had a slate to write on. A book of saints to read. She could do it on the ground: write, draw a few scribbles, with a stick. They glanced at each other, she and Yellow. What she drew on the ground, when you looked at it, could have been a cow. The other, the real one, was calm today, enjoying the grass. About time. The girl thought about something she'd heard the previous night. How a cow can feed her calf even after she has died. She keeps a trickle of milk going for a whole day. How old are you, Yellow? How many children? When I was born, you were already here. They said then you were capricious. Don't deny it.

It was good to talk to the cows. To know how to talk to them. It was good for the animals. And good for the humans. For cowgirls, it was a way of killing time, loneliness, fear. And irritation. Carme got over her fear of the mountain with an errand her father gave her. She had to take a bundle of bread and food. She had to leave it on a rock, in a crevice. Who's it for? That doesn't matter. It's for someone who needs it. If you're stopped by the guards, all you have to do is say, 'It's mine.' Not another word. Another day, she took a jug of milk. When she came back the following day, the jug was empty. Poor people, not only were they invisible, but they were also hungry. Going back to cows, it was easy to run out of patience, truth be told. One day, a storyteller named Xan das Bolas came to the dance hall in Tabeaio. He was already famous for his roles as a nightwatchman and a civil guard in several films. He can't have been a bad comedian, since in a sequence of *Historias de la radio* he played the role of a sergeant in the civil guard, being hoisted onto people's shoulders. The day after his stellar performance in Tabeaio, it was the turn of Pepa, my mother's younger sister, to pasture the cows. And she addressed them. She gave them a courageous speech. No muttering under her breath, no sweet nothings.

'I'm going to be a bohemian!'

It was a strange word, waiting for its turn, and this is why it came out so naturally. From Dona Isabel's factory of synonyms for naming the forbidden, perhaps.

'I've had enough of you!' shouted Pepa in her discourse to the cows. 'I'm going to be a bohemian. And a film star. I'm going to elope with Xan das Bolas!'

Pepa must have been about eight. Her discourse reached the ears of Dona Isabel, who had an extraordinary information service. This Dona Isabel was the parish priest's niece and lived with him in the Big House in Corpo Santo. Next to it was the small, humble abode of the Barrós family, bursting with children. Eight of them managed to survive, four girls and four boys – whichever way you looked at it, a lot of mouths for a widower. So Dona Isabel formed a kind of protectorate for them, albeit provisional and open to the whims of fate. It would seem my mother, Carme, was her favourite. Because she was quiet. This was true. My mother was quiet because she talked to herself. And was never a bother. When she wasn't working, she would shut herself up in the attic to read the lives of saints. She would enter that dark chamber and seek a ray of light between the tiles to feed her clandestine happiness: the literature of lives that were extreme, unusual, radical, extraordinary. They may have been saints, but what she read – or the way she read them – was the lives of unrestrained, bewitching women, and strange men with 'wind in their branches'.

Carme was never a problem. She did her work without complaint. She went from the cowshed, from milking the cows, to the attic with her saints.

What Pepa had said, however, was very worrying. She was the smallest, and she'd stood gazing at the road and talked about leaving.

'She said she was going to elope with Xan das Bolas!' shrieked Dona Isabel to my grandfather.

'With Xan das Bolas?'

She was an enigmatic woman, as devout as she was romantic, as repressed as she was passionate. She felt drawn towards my grandfather and at the same time obliged to stay away. God had been considerate towards her, but had not equipped her with the grace of humour.

'A little girl's joke,' said my grandfather. 'Don't give it importance.'

But she was used to ruling. Her own life, and the lives of others.

'Even so, it would be better for the girl not to go with the cows anymore.'

Not far from Corpo Santo, in a place called Castelo, was another cowgirl, Manuela, who would later marry Francisco, one of my mother's brothers. Francisco may have had worn patches on his trousers – he was a poor fellow – yet he was heavily contested in every household. In all the houses, there was a welcome and a seat for Francisco. Because Francisco, be he poor or not, was a gift. To start with, he could catch trout in the river by hand. And stories as well. By hand. As they flew past. He had various jobs,

María and Aunt Pepa

but this one, telling stories, kept him going. He worked in a shoe factory that belonged to the Senra family, a family with a long Republican tradition. It was later confiscated. He then became a barber.

I have already spoken about him. He retired some time ago. Even so, at the age of ninety, old clients still solicit his presence at home, in an old people's home, in hospital. Francisco resists, but ends up going. With his vanity case. Scissors and comb. And memory. The vanity case of memory. Words. Because he knows he hasn't been called for his skill as a hairdresser. What they want is to listen to him. And if he has his scissors with him, well, so much the better, for dotting the suspense. A tap of the scissors. There is the inflection. The unforeseen.

The scissors slice through the air. One moment. Time to rewind.

The king of the mountains was O Xalo. When night falls, it has the disposition of a wild, stubborn land that wants to see the sea again. It's still an impressive mountain, but back then it was even more so. There were no tarmacked roads, nor had half its back been built on. It was a mountain that allowed you, or refused to allow you, to pass. Every time, you had to find a way through. And that was where Manuela stepped on the sun.

She was eight. Her two brothers had been recruited for the war. So it was her turn – there was nobody else – to drive the cattle to pasture. The cows, two oxen and a horse.

'Go to O Xalo. There's plenty of grazing. They'll run free, more or less. You won't have to watch where they're stepping.'

'How long for?'

'Come back when you step on the sun.'

However much she asked, she couldn't work out how she was going to step on the sun. Until the time came. She spent the whole afternoon waiting. On tenterhooks. With an eye on the sun. How she was going to step on it. Until the moment arrived, and it was really quite simple. The sun was at her feet. And so she stepped on it.

What she never got over was lightning. She was terrified of thunderstorms. Especially when she became a seamstress. A travelling seamstress. She'd learned how to sew when she was fourteen, on a Singer. She tried sewing at home, but it hardly made her prosperous. She often got paid in kind. You do my clothes, and I'll give you some eggs. Some potatoes. Some flour. But nothing like the day when a photographer, in order to pay for what she'd done for his daughters, did a session for her. Not one photograph. A whole session.

If the orders didn't come or there weren't that many, then she'd have to go looking for them. She and a friend, María, decided to become travelling seamstresses. They carried a portable Singer on their heads from village to village. Over mountains and valleys. Down paths and deep tracks. Sometimes, a third friend would join them. It didn't matter how well the friend could sew. When she sang, it was the same as with the lark. Which scatters all fear. Grabs hold of clouds, thunder and lightning. This girl sang so well she ended up fronting various dance orchestras and along the coast of A Coruña became a star, much admired, by the name of Finita Gay. Until she boarded a ship to make her fortune in America.

Manuela carried on with her portable sewing machine for a while. From village to village. One day, she met Francisco along the way. He didn't sing to banish the bolts of lightning. He distracted them with his stories. They all fell and thundered somewhere else, on the mountain of O Xalo, where barefoot cowgirls step on the sun.

6

The Sky's Ruins

For a time, having come back from Venezuela, my father worked in the village of O Rego, the place in Sigrás where he was raised, doing up the family home, and he took us with him. When the repair work began, we slept in a shed that was attached to one side of the house. On a wooden floor you got to by climbing a staircase. There was no electric light, just volumes of shadows and aromas. María and I, sharing a bed, on a corn-husk mattress. We had slept in humble farmhouses, feeling the caress of the stone next to our pillows, hearing the scurrying of mice in the attic, the strange creaking of beds that brought sighs from the marital bedrooms or the shuffling of an old man and the shell-like sound of the chamber pot, the willow fighting with the wind on the window, the ebb and flow of the dogs' warning barks. This was something different, new. Intense sensations activate all the senses. The inner senses – the current of memory – and the outer ones. But there are times when all the senses rely on one. That summer night in the loft, all the senses, having done their work, converged on sight. In the old roof, not far from our bed, there were gaps, missing tiles. But they didn't seem dangerous, rather a deliberate act on the part of the ruins. They were windows to the firmament. We'd never seen the sky so close before. The stars, so trusting.

Stretched out, covered by a blanket, not talking, we forgot to worry about the rudimentary bed, the veins of the husks printed on our bodies, perhaps because everything was getting lighter, airborne and luminous, with a glow we hadn't seen before, which spread slowly through the dark room, landing on our faces with the texture of mill dust. If María didn't say a word, if María slept with her eyes open, if María was blue in the night, like the cobwebs, the apples and the bales of hay, then I would be the same. It was only for a few nights. We never said anything. Not even to each other. We never complained. Our mother would have got annoyed, demanded alternative accommodation. We kept the starry roof in the pocket of our darkness. The night adopted us. Revealed itself to us. In a way, we would always be part of its lineage.

'Weren't you afraid?'

'Not at all!'

'These two can sleep with their eyes open,' said my father.

'Are they barn owls?' asked my father's cousin, staring at us.

'Real barn owls.'

The young man then mimicked the call of the barn owl. A screech that pierced the day and night. He was a barn owl too.

They treated us well. The village, for children from the city, was one long party. Especially if something abnormal happened to you. For example, if you were wounded.

The two young men who did most of the work for that farming family in Sigrás adopted me as a mascot for their tireless team. I always travelled like a king. On the cart. On horseback. One of the jobs that season was to plough, harrow, and finally level the ground with a levelling board. This was a glorious moment for me. The levelling board was a frame set with thick osiers. Drawn by animals, it acted like a comb that levelled the ground the plough had already softened. So that it didn't slide over the surface or take off because of the drawing power of a pair of oxen, the levelling board was weighed down with stones. And on top of the stones went the child. It wasn't the closest thing to a dream. It *was* a dream. To climb on a mat or trolley pulled by oxen and to travel on a stone throne over the unending expanse of black earth. The unfamiliar adventure was also the child's first experience of a certain power. Being transported by those mythological creatures that obeyed the friendly voices. But the child also abruptly learned that animals, even the meekest oxen, don't enjoy work and are dying to throw off the yoke as soon as they can. Despite the ballast of child and stones, the cattle noticed the lightness and gave a sudden jerk. Because of the abrupt movement, the child fell off and was hurt by one of the stones. He had blood on his knee. Red blood with a white streak, strangely enough. He didn't like this at all. The two young men rescued him, carried him in the air, running along shortcuts, and all three fell as they jumped over a wall. What he remembers is that, instead of heightening the drama, this made them burst out laughing. And the more one laughed, the more the other laughed. The child didn't know what to think. So he burst out laughing as well.

When they reached the houses, the bleeding had stopped. And formed a scab. It looked good on the child's leg.

'He's going to stay with us in the village forever. He's going to be a wild thing!'

More laughter. What to do? You had to read everything they said back to front.

My father told me the story of a wild man. Perhaps so that I would know what a wild man was really like. His name was Ganzo.

He met a girl, and they fell in love. He would come down from the mountains, from a more isolated village. On horseback. Her father didn't approve of the relationship. He suspected that his daughter was disobeying him and locked her up at home. He was always on the lookout. Here was a man who wielded a stick, with a reputation for being very harsh. He also had a shotgun. Not an easy man to stand up to. Every Sunday, Ganzo would come down and plant himself in front of their house, motionless for hours and hours, staring at the front door. Night would fall, and he would leave. Nobody ever came out to talk to him. But the following week he would be back. One day, the door opened and the girl's father emerged with a weapon.

'What do you want, Ganzo?'

And he replied with a historic command:

'Release the captive!'

The girl's father was deeply affected, perplexed. This man from the mountains had shown him up in front of everybody.

Sometimes, when I'm writing, I am reminded of this story. The ending. Those surprising words, which were said in Spanish with medieval brio. The precise use of the delicate term 'captive'. I mentioned it to him one day. My father clicked his tongue. Gazed at some indeterminate point in the distance.

'That's not what he said.'

'Oh, really?'

'Really.'

He saw the disappointment in my eyes. I understood we were studying the same subject matter in our own, different ways. On the borders of truth and fiction.

'What did Ganzo say?'

He looked at me. He was about to say it. He smiled inwardly. Didn't say anything.

'You have to tell me,' I pleaded with him.

'It would be better to drop it.'

'What did he say?'

He seemed now to hesitate, not between fact and invention, but between two realities.

'*Let the bitch go!* That's what he said.'

'*The bitch?*'

'Yes. It seems that's what he said.'

'The other one was better.'

We were sitting on the porch. There was a plant that had drawn his attention. How quickly it grew. Its jubilant green colour. He was also on the verge of saying something about that plant, but he never did. It was a cannabis plant sown by María.

'I'll tell you what happened,' he said, with reference to Ganzo. 'One heard one thing, another heard another.'

'But what do you think he said?'

'I don't know. The girl's father shot at his feet to frighten him away. But he stayed where he was. He didn't flinch. I heard the shot. That much is certain.'

After one village, there was another, more distant village, which was the former's remote place, the last frontier, but after this village there would be another, and another that had its own remote marker, in a geographical chain towards the unknown, which was a kind of imaginary reverse. In reality, everything formed a mental geography, a dense confederation of villages, an unending intersection of roads. The remote place might be an hour's walk away. I remember that the first pilgrimage we ever went on, from Corpo Santo to San Bieito, was a long way. It was very hot, and by the sides of the road there were cherry trees that offered shade and fruit. We couldn't reach the branches, but the adults gave us some to eat. They were happy, and so were we. Processions were always something more than just a Mass. They were a party that transformed the day. Suddenly the sides of the road converged into a corridor of bodies and groans. Cripples. Blind people. Disfigured faces. Women in mourning with babies on their bosoms. I'd seen people begging before, but not in such a choral way. I was impressed by the psalmody of their voices and above all, at a child's height, by the mute expression, the fixed gaze, of their stumps. The rite of healing, exorcism or protection in San Bieito involved passing through a hole in a stone wall. For children it was easy, but not for an adult. If the adult was fat, seeing him there, half his body on one side and half on the other, was comical to begin with. But misfortune – if it's going to be funny – mustn't last. Losing one's balance and falling over. Slipping on the pavement. A slap that knocks the other over. A pie in the face. One's trousers falling down. All of this is funny if it doesn't last. When someone is trying to pass from one side to another, through a gap in the wall, and this is a holy, curative rite, and it's obvious he can't, he gets trapped, his face becomes sweaty and distorted, it's like witnessing the comical and its reverse at one and the same time. The miracle doesn't exist, but its defeat does. The flailing arms of the carnal metaphor. Everybody pushing, the encouraging voices, would sometimes ensure a successful passage, and the body would collapse on the far side, like someone falling onto the grass of the imagination. Relief would sweep through the crowd. A general comforting of people and stones. Relief. That must be the closest thing to a miracle.

No, San Bieito wasn't far. But it was for me. It was the first time I saw a blind man with one eye that laughed and another that cried. The hole in the stone united ailments and parties, whoops and groans, petitions and sky rockets, dawn and dusk. And the image of the wall, like a border with the beyond, with its round passage, like a curative, but also a sarcastic and occasionally cruel eye. I ended up realising San Bieito was part of a country that was both invisible and omnipresent. A cobweb blown and transfixed by the wind of history, but not broken. Many of our first trips, aside from family visits, were to sacred places which appeared on the calendar as feast days. Pilgrimages, at least part of which one did on foot. Today, if allowed to, cars will penetrate and profane even the fairground. There's a reason for going on foot. With a votive offering on one's head. To give time to the sacred. This is the time for approaching what is eccentric. When I write, I go on foot. Determined, content, with a cherry from time to time. Until the legs start trembling because over there is the wall. And the hole in the wall.

Sometimes, one doesn't arrive, and that's because of not going on foot. This happened the last time I went to Santo André de Teixido, the most eccentric and possibly the most authentic pilgrimage. By car. In the company of Liz Nash, a British writer and journalist, the whole way talking to her about the saint who came by sea in a stone boat. Explaining the meaning of this expression, 'stone boat', which refers to the type of ballast. Interpreting the legend that says whoever doesn't go to Teixido when alive will go when he has died. The reason for not killing animals, even insects, since they could be deceased people on the road. The idea of re-existence, the transmigration of souls, in popular knowledge. And so on.

Until we get to the sanctuary. The sun sets the sea ablaze, while expert nature prepares a beautiful sunset for the last remaining pilgrims. At the side door of the temple is a priest in a cassock and clerical collar. It's the end of the day for him too. Liz goes to talk to him and asks for his interpretation of the

50

legend. Through the half-open door can be seen the pale anatomies of wax votive offerings, like broken toys waiting for a miracle. She's really very interested. It's fascinating to come across a living belief in the transmigration of souls – such an oriental philosophy – at the far end of Western Europe. The priest takes a swig. Glances over at me. Gazes at the sea. At Liz.

He clicks his tongue.

Says, 'Old wives' tales!'

Now that's a wild man.

7

The Saxophone's Farewell

My father never travelled by plane. He had already seen the face of that strange aviator and been warned about aviation.

By train, he travelled often. Especially when he was young. On the roof of the carriage. He regarded the day he was told he was going to work as a bricklayer's mate on a building site in A Coruña as a kind of liberation. Unlike in that story by Clarín, '¡Adiós, Cordera!', in my father's story the cow was the one who was sad, while my father's heart leapt for joy the day he left the green prison of the meadows behind. He never missed his time as a herdsman. And he certainly would have had no interest in being described as a 'friend of animals'. Despite the headbutt that occurred during the aeronautical episode, it wasn't a question of fear or hatred. He almost always kept a polite, but non-negotiable distance from them, even if they were pets. The most notable exception was Knuckle, a small, long-tailed mongrel who could not be described as being so clever, all he had to do was talk. I am one of those who think that animals talk, but we don't understand them. What made Knuckle different was that you *could* understand a large part of what he was saying. He expressed himself with great sincerity, albeit with a hint of irony. In my father's opinion, he wasn't exactly a person. He was something else: a personage. During the long winter evenings, they would watch television together. They also shared an enjoyment of music. For my father, humankind's greatest achievement was a band of jazz musicians.

'They play like God!'

Knuckle died soon after I started working as a journalist. I wrote an article in which I shared a concern raised by my mother: can an animal like Knuckle go to heaven? The surprising thing was that, a few days later, a wise theologian, Andrés Torres Queiruga, replied by saying, 'Why ever not?' Animals had souls. And there was no reason for humans to be left alone in the beyond. My mother cut out the article, and it was one of the things she kept in her bedside table while she was alive.

It came time to slaughter the pig, and my father did the opposite of most people. He disappeared.

The little house in Castro de Elviña, where we went to live in 1963, was in a remote place known as Nacha Mount, next to a dirt track that led up to O Escorial and the broadcasting tower of Radio Coruña. One of the first nuggets of information I gleaned, with dismay, from locals was that this summit was where the wind turned around. A quality that is attributed to many summits, but in this case – and all you had to do was hear the sullen roar of the eucalyptuses – seemed much more realistic. It wasn't just one or two witnesses who said this. Everybody made the same remark: 'You're going to live where the wind turns around!' That business of watching the wind change direction was something that kept me occupied – and preoccupied – for quite some time. Especially when my father declared, 'The city will never reach here!' There was some truth in this. The seagulls from A Coruña always turned back here, at the *ne plus ultra* of the enormous radio tower, even when it was stormy. The starlings did the same, drawing sudden cartoons in the sky. But the crows didn't. The crows flew high overhead, on their own or in ragged formation, and then suddenly swooped down or soared towards the unknown. I rather liked the crows. In church, always damp and cold, our bodies petrified like the rest of the temple, there was a point at which we revived, and it was when the priest read that part in the Book of Genesis with the episode about Noah's Ark. Everybody watching the priest's hands as he mimics the action of releasing the dove and the raven with their mission as meteorological informers after the flood. The dove came back with an olive leaf in its beak, but nothing else was ever said about the crow. Whatever happened to it? Of course, it never came back. All you had to do was see it up there, on our mountain. Roaming free. The dove is a journalist. The crow, that vagabond, is a poet. The cuckoo as well. The cuckoo also continued with its journey. I never heard the cuckoo so clearly again. One of the few times my grandfather the carpenter broke his silence was to tell me a proverb slowly, like someone distilling a haiku: 'If the cuckoo doesn't sing in March or April, either the cuckoo is dead or the end is coming.' There was a large rock that bore its name and had its shape, a winged stone bird whose beak pointed in the direction of the lighthouse. A rock that was about to fly, this was its position. Every year, in March or April, the cuckoo came by. It was on its way north from some-where in Africa. There must have been a saga of African cuckoos following the same path. It was obvious the route was intentional because the cuckoo didn't hurry past. It cuckooed for a while, growing louder and softer. All our desire focused on our sight, on wanting to see the cuckoo. A Zapateira back then was an unending expanse of mystery, a no man's land inhabited, for us, by imaginary creatures that sometimes came visiting in the shape of a fox, a rabbit, a weasel or a barn owl. It was also the first place the cuckoo sang. There was still no road there, no golf club. Until the road and the golf course were built. And Franco's retinue arrived in summer, the whole mountain bristling with hundreds of guards. Up high, we were never sure whether the wind jostled the crows, their ragged flight, or the crows directed the wind.

My father couldn't stand the pig slaughter, or that of any other animal. He would build the sheds, the pens, the cages – that small, domestic farm around our garden. He would help to raise them. He built the bath, that trough where the pig was preserved in salt. The pig slaughter used to take place during St Martin's summer, under the November sun. It was a day of great festivity in every household. In popular Galician culture, which is so Pantagruelian, the pig is a providential source of nourishment, so to speak. There is the eloquent image of a local who is asked his favourite bird and looks up at the sky to exclaim, 'If only pigs could fly!' There are lots of laudatory proverbs, and they aren't always that old. Like the one that says, 'The pig has saved more people than penicillin.' But my father would disappear that day. He didn't want to know anything about the slaughter. His horror was not even modified by a desire for revenge. When he was self-employed, he would sometimes go months without getting paid. After such periods of abstinence, sometimes the whole lot would come along at once. The house was isolated. An easy target for thieves. Things would get stolen some Sundays when we weren't there. There wasn't that much to take. The point is, one Saturday my father got paid for the work of several months. The next day we were invited to a family gathering. Where to keep the money? The idea was brilliant. He put the peseta notes in an empty paint pot. A metal pot with a secure lid he hid in the pigsty, beneath the undergrowth that served as bedding. He shut the door with a padlock. The idea was brilliant. Who would ever think of such a hiding place? When we came back in the evening, the padlock was still in place. He opened the door. The first thing he saw was the pot. Without its lid, and with nothing inside. The pig had rooted and rooted until it found the pieces of paper. In a flash, the animal had gobbled down the work of months. But my father didn't go to that slaughter either.

One of my uncles would carry out the task of killing the pig. The labours that followed were performed like a rite: scorching the skin with torches, washing it, opening it, cutting it into pieces, salting it. My mother took care of all the preparations. She also found the arms to hold the animal down. The role of executioner was not imbued with any ritual content or artistic display. It was just a question of killing. Identifying the fastest route to the heart and sticking the knife in. Quickly, but carefully. I remember being there when they made the cut to collect the flow of blood in a bowl. And to stir the blood, which would go to making blood sausages, so it didn't coagulate.

My father's absence was never remarked on. It was simply ignored. It was just a strange thing, and there you go. Like belonging to another religion.

My mother took care of the other sacrifices, the poultry and rabbits. It wasn't her vocation to be a butcher, she did it to give us something to eat. Someone had to do it. One of the worst days of her life was when a beheaded duck wriggled free. The bird carried on flying for a while above our heads. She tried to calm herself down, as well as us: 'Poor thing! It had a lot of electricity.'

We avoided the theme of sacrifice, but sometimes it turned up unexpectedly and not in the best place. At the table. As happened with the baritone cockerel. It woke us every morning. Time went by. My mother postponed the fatal moment. Until, having given us prior warning, she prepared it for a feast day. We knew she was hurting the most. She wandered about on her own, saying, 'This is it. Never again!' My father didn't eat that day. All of us chewing a musical scale with the rice. From time to time, years later, my father would remember the singer:

'That cockerel was worth a *potosí*!'

This was the maximum value my father could assign to anything. A *potosí* was what the saxophone was worth as well.

My father learned to read music before books. Music theory before his ABC. He learned a few letters, he spent several months at school, but to read and write properly he used his free time doing military service in the barracks in Parga. He was in the band, and it was so cold in winter he used to say, 'The notes hung frozen in the air.' According to him, during that glacial period, a cornet got stuck to a note one night and couldn't be prised away from the lips. We all laughed at this exaggeration, and he said, 'You're laughing out of ignorance.' He was right. The old army barracks in Parga, abandoned today, the huts covered in brambles, fills the eyes with cold, even if you observe it from afar in summer. That boy who from the age of twelve would run from Sigrás to Cambre Bridge, like so many others, to jump on the trains and go to work in the city, by a happy coincidence would learn to play the saxophone. My grandfather the carpenter got him an instrument in exchange for some work he'd done. Manuel worked on site and then attended lessons with a teacher who made a living playing the piano in a nightclub in A Coruña.

From his life as a bricklayer's mate, my father always recalled the day it occurred to him to heat twenty-four workmen's pots using some teak planks. They produced a wonderful fire, all embers, no smoke. He was amazed. The building site was in O Recheo. He didn't realise this wood was worth almost a *potosí* and the site owner, when he turned up in his white shoes, let fly a curse that shook all the branches in Méndez Núñez Gardens. He expressed his intention aloud: 'I'm going to barbecue that bricklayer's mate!' That day, with the help of his colleagues, my father also disappeared.

He got out of that situation and others. In time, he would make a good builder. Even though, when he was young, the thing he loved best was the saxophone. For years, he combined both jobs – his salary as a builder with his weekend performances at open-air dances and in dance halls. Musicians in A Coruña would congregate around the bar La Tacita de Plata. This is where he met the real heroes of popular emotions. Those who kept the

The author's father, the saxophonist

spaces of romance and partying open during that wretched period. He played in prearranged and spontaneous orchestras. This was when musicians got hired by village mayors or the owners of dance halls. The decline of the dance hall, that is what set many musicians back. It was the life of a sparrow. In summer, grain; in winter, the inferno. My father never abandoned his job as a builder. Like the sparrow, he was afraid of winter. As children, we watched him leave with his saxophone after work. He would climb on board a wagon with the other members of the orchestra, often on his way to a remote place, in lands that bordered on León and Asturias. Until that unbearable rhythm got the better of him, like Chaplin in *Modern Times*, dancing sleepily on an unstoppable machine.

The builder, the professional amateur, abandoned music. But the saxophone remained. For us children and our mother, it was the house's secret treasure, dozing in its case on top of the wardrobe, awaiting better times. The saxophone would occasionally come down and alight in my father's hands. The last time we heard it was at a party on Christmas Eve. My father played paso dobles, boleros and even the odd Christmas carol. My mother killed herself laughing. That evening, I understood, I thought I saw, when and why they fell in love. Here was a man transformed, creating harmonies.

Early one evening, my father arrived in the company of a man with a moustache that formed a kind of horseshoe around his mouth. He was stocky, but trailed his arms, as if he bore the weight of an anatomical tiredness. There was something decadent about him. Both of them were very serious. Silent. My father entered the master bedroom and took the saxophone case down from the wardrobe. We cried. It just happened. María and I started crying. It was a lament for which there was no consolation. The feeling that all the clocks of all times had been broken. My father wasn't expecting this sense of solidarity with the old saxophone. He stood there, looking perplexed and disturbed. He called us over and said in a serious voice:

'Do you know why I'm giving it to him? He needs it to make a living.'

We cried, yes, but I think the saddest thing was that man with the dark eyes and the horseshoe moustache. We watched him leave with the black case. Suddenly, he turned around to face us. He put his hand in his pocket and gave us a twenty-five-peseta coin. He then walked down the hill, in the dusk, his body listing to one side, like someone leading a soul by the hand.

8

The Journey to Restless Paradise

The first image is that of an old woman dressed in mourning in the window. But she's not looking at me. I follow the direction of her gaze, and there is a busy man. It's Farruco, lining up his shoes and boots on top of a wall. He cleans them, polishes them with bitumen or horse fat, and makes them shine with a cloth and brush. He then orders them in pairs, according to their age. There are the shoes of a lifetime, in the Sunday sun.

Gaston Bachelard defined the world painted by Chagall as a 'restless paradise'. I didn't know anything then about Bachelard's poetic philosophy or Chagall's uneasy village, but I knew this place as a child and grew up there. A paradise where colourful horses ate thorns; harsh, with the name of a battlefield, but true. It was Castro de Elviña.

My father was happy to have built there, with his own hands, what he called in the Venezuelan style a *ranchito*. A one-storey house on the hillside. He chose to fit the door, which my grandfather had made, on the day of the great snowfall of 1963. He crossed the Monelos river and the railway with the door on his back. There were three of us: my grandfather the carpenter carrying the frame; my father with the door; and the child bringing up the rear, holding a tool, counting their footsteps and trying to step in their footprints. My father had to do it. He had to place the laurel on top. He had to have his own home. But his most precise definition of independence was the following: 'You have to live somewhere where you can't hear the neighbour pulling the chain.'

To begin with, Carme, my sister María and I were not at all convinced by this biblical exodus from Monte Alto to another, even taller mountain at the end of a dirt track, with torrents of rainwater and lacking any public transport. To get to the city, you had to cover a large distance across open country to reach the Avenue (Alfonso Molina) and then wait for the Cockroach, the bus that came from the coast, full of people, and did justice to the song 'La Cucaracha', which was often sung by the passengers: 'The cockroach, the cockroach / can no longer walk / because he doesn't have, because he lacks / four back wheels.' Very near the bus stop, they had just inaugurated the Coca-Cola factory that would supply the whole of Galicia. A remarkable building for its time, it was a huge glass cube next to the road, surrounded by nature. While waiting for the Cockroach finally to arrive in a splutter, we would gaze in amazement at the unceasing movement of the conveyor belt, where rows of bottles of the potion would enter one side empty and come out the other full, without the presence, so far as we could tell, of any human being. When they talk to me about magical realism, that literary label so abused by lazy critics, the first thing that comes to my mind is that transparent factory and the vision of the bottles filling up on their own, while we waited for the ancient, heaving bus with its embittered engine. The way the Cockroach moved, that was realism. And there was something magical about it too.

Castro de Elviña women

We'd had to leave Marola Street in a hurry, a rapid evacuation. The owners wanted the ground floor for something else and gave us no notice. I remember my mother went to discuss a moratorium with them. She took me along with her. She was very calm, but that day I could feel her racing pulse in her hand. We were received in the hallway by the wife. She was a stiff, bejewelled kind of woman. My mother said something similar to Rosalía de Castro's poem 'Justice by the Hand'. The woman called out for her husband. We were surprised to see a little man in an apron. The woman tried to incite him against my mother, but he quivered and spoke in a whisper. It wasn't clear who or what he was more afraid of – the irate tenant or his wife's commands. In the end, Carme stared at this stuttering figure, took me by the hand, and we left without another word. On the way back, she kept talking to herself. All I could feel now on the palm of my mother's hand was the fuming of her *sirvente*.

While my father got going with the work on the house, on that patch of hillside he'd bought with the help of his Venezuelan bolivars, we stayed for several months with my paternal grandparents, the carpenter and the seamstress. They also lived on a mountain, next to O Birloque and A Cabana, in O Martinete, a place of which almost no trace is left. My grandfather worked away from home, but had a workshop on the ground floor of the house and, on Sundays, would cultivate a field next to the Monelos river, which flowed through the fertile land of A Granxa and into the port of A Coruña. Back then, the river was still alive. If eels swam up it, it was because they remembered the thousands of years the little Monelos had meandered through Os Sargazos. Since then, the river has also disappeared and been buried. It crosses the city in a pipe and merges with the sea without anybody noticing. Sometimes, during a downpour, you can hear the mutter, the roar, of the river's ghost in an underground garage.

One of those who lived in O Martinete was a mute man with a long beard. I think his name was Fidel, or that was what they called him, possibly with reference to the Cuban revolution. He was a good friend of my grandfather the carpenter. The two of them got on very well in silence. Fidel the sawmill operator always wore blue overalls and really did resemble a legendary hero. He had the air of an Argonaut who'd lost the power of speech on an island where words are stolen. He was both thickset and nimble, and put all his body into making signs whenever he wanted to convey something. Needless to say, he was the most communicative neighbour for miles around. My grandfather would listen with his eyes and then become thoughtful or nod. They could be like this for hours. He was a whole, philosophising anatomy, exclaiming with his eyelids, emphasising with his eyebrows and writing in the air with his arms or hands, his fingers composing ideograms. One day, the fountain stopped working. No water emerged from the spout. The mute, who understood all about machinery, started to explain the problem to the huddle of neighbours. He didn't use words but, judging by the attention they paid, you could see the extraordinary eloquence, the energy, of his talking body. The way he drew the water's path in the air. The law of communicating vessels. When he'd finished, the water started flowing out of the spout. It couldn't do otherwise. Nobody needed any more convincing. It would have been a shame for the water not to emerge.

And then the day of the great snowfall arrived. The day for carrying the door. For having our own home.

This is the area where the University of A Coruña now stands. It should really be called the University of Castro de Elviña. That was one of the first things they taught me. Castro was one thing, A Coruña another. In this area, where everybody hankers after the city's coat of arms, Castro is the only place known to have defended its position as a village. This is what happened when the first neighbourhood association was constituted. The meeting took place in Leonor's pub. The governor, at a time when governors were like a panoptic eye that watched over everything, dispatched a plain-clothes policeman. He didn't need to introduce himself. He was the only one dressed in a suit and tie. The secret man took a seat and started noting down everything that was said. At one point, however, he stopped writing, and that was when the assembly unanimously agreed to remain as a 'village', rejecting the term 'city district'. A woman, who warned she'd left a saucepan on the stove, then intervened to protest against a tax for the cleaning of chimneys. Had anybody ever laid eyes on this municipal chimney sweep? Might the long-awaited, real chimney sweep not be that man, the one taking notes? The civil servant was nonplussed. He grabbed his notes and scurried away like a nervous, frustrated detective afraid of a place that is not so much dangerous as imaginary.

We realised we'd reached a breeding ground on land as soon as we arrived. We were about to put down roots in a territory that seemed hostile. Dogs ran free and snapped at our outsider heels. María and I didn't dare set foot outside the precinct. The only thing that calmed us down that night was spotting the beam of the lighthouse. It was further away now, but this meant you could see it better. Its circular glow penetrated the dusk and entered through our window. When we woke up and went outside, we saw the whole mountain had been painted in colours. The washerwomen had spread out their clothes. And the Barreiro girls, Pepe and Maruxa's daughters, were atop the Cuckoo's Crag. Among other things, we learned that carnival was coming. And on Shrove Tuesday, at the football stadium, something would happen that had never happened before.

'What's that?'

'There'll be women playing!' said Beatriz.

If women were playing football, then clearly we weren't in the back of beyond. It was true the wind turned around here. How could it not? It was at the service of the washerwomen.

9

The Weatherman

I saw him dig two wells. He probably dug others. Real wells, artesian wells, for the supply of water. Even though this wasn't his job. On the contrary. My father's work as a builder was more closely linked with height than depth. But when it was necessary, he would open a hole in the ground. And start building downwards.

He worked for a long time with Xosé, a younger man who called him 'master'. Xosé of Vilamouro was very serious, very quiet, and while he worked only ever expressed himself with deep onomatopoeias and the experimental music of tools in action. I was struck by the way he addressed my father as 'master' and did it so naturally. This meant there was a master doing the same job, which implied not a hierarchy, but respect. In this case, the master was my father. There are words that fill the look. I could argue with my father, be in disagreement, get annoyed, but, whenever he was working, I couldn't help viewing him as a master. The builder's silence, like that of other trades, has to do with the need to hear the sound of his work. The sound produced by the tools entering into contact with the material. A lack of harmony reveals a fault in the symmetry. You have to hear the trowel or the ruler when you plaster a wall. But, on animated occasions, the opposite process can take place. Now Xosé and my father are humming, whistling, trumpet and sax, in comes the trombone, the music affects the tools, filling them with a desire for style. Perhaps in this as well, my father, who learned music theory before his ABC, is playing the role of master. When something in the material rebels, when the mass disobeys, he falls silent. Looks around, examines the disharmony. Checks the mixture. Proceeds over the fault. Doesn't swear or curse. I know what he's going to say . . .

'Cymbals, Manuel! Let the wonders of the world ignite!'

When he was working near home, I would take him his lunch in an earthenware pot with the lid tied down by a strip of tyre. They almost always kept a bonfire going on site, from which they would remove some embers to heat the pot. That fire had a special smell. A fire on site smells of the building site. They generally

The author's father on the left

use bits of plank from the moulds. Damp, covered in lumps of cement. Fire doesn't like them. It starts emitting smoke. What keeps the flames going, what revives them and gives them meaning, is the thick paper from the sacks of cement. The flames rise and fall sulkily. It's important the way the paper, splinters and planks are positioned. A pyramid with the correct amount of air flowing through it. But this reticence makes the flames more long-lasting. It's a fire that's difficult to put out, even if it's raining. When it was very cold, they would build a primitive stove, burning sawdust in a metal drum that was also used for preparing whitewash. I liked the smell of the building site. The fragrance of cold, hard, headstrong materials. Until the structure had been built, the materials would occupy the site with a sullen identity. The heap of sand smelled of the sea. In those days, they fetched sand from the beaches or dunes. It had to be sieved. What filtered through was fine sand like flour. What didn't filter through were crumbs of the sea's memory, bits of shell, of sea urchin, a crab's pincer. On the lookout and bad-tempered, the iron, wood, bricks, blocks, asbestos, tiles, slates. This is why the bonfire was important, however poor it might be. It was like a sign or an ownerless dog that refused to budge from the empty site. After two or three weeks, everything was different, the materials had adopted a different disposition. A state of cheerfulness. The bricks weighed less. The pulley wheels squeaked. The spirit level and plumb line legislated over the void.

When it comes to building, there are jobs that are imbued with a certain aura. The job of painter, for example. My father could immediately tell who the carpenter, electrician or plumber was. He had no problem identifying the painter. It was obvious from the haircut, the shirt, the style. What about the builder? The builder is the one who puts everything together where there was nothing before, the one who places the laurel on top. There's a roof, a house. But there's something wrong with being a builder.

'Become a painter. They sing on site. They're good to work with. And they wear shirts that give off light.'

Xosé used to laugh at this business with the shirts. Perhaps that was the problem with builders. They didn't dare put on a loud shirt. I wanted to be a lorry driver. I had great admiration for a friend of my father, Jorge from Palavea. He used to wear bright shirts as well. But when the lorry broke down, he would remove his shirt and slide under the machine with a naked torso. He didn't come out until he'd fixed it. He referred to his lorry as a large, strong, good, but slightly deranged animal. Which broke down for the most absurd reasons. Once, after hours of fishing around, he came out from under the lorry, complaining vociferously, and showed me a steel ball bearing. Glinting in the sun. See this? It had a black spot, like a tiny amount of decay on the enamel of a tooth.

He was sweaty. Grimy. He stared at the lorry's snout in dismay. The way they behaved, they resembled each other more and more closely.

'That's the reason it stopped. Do you find that normal?'

The way they related to their tools. This was another detail that caught my attention whenever I visited the site and observed Xosé and my father. They felt a responsibility towards them, which they never shirked. The day only came to a close when they'd cleaned and washed the tools. They did this meticulously, leaving not a single stain. Their hands would grow soft, pale, all wrinkled, like skinless creatures, while the tools would regain a modest splendour and lie down in a resting position, as in a dormitory. Until tomorrow.

In some part of my brain, in the secret Department of

Essential Information, is the day my father explained to me the purpose of a plumb line and, in particular, of the air bubble in the tube of a spirit level. The house is supported by the air bubble, that one right there. The bubble sees a lot better than your eye. The bubble has information about terrestrial coordinates, meridians and parallels. The bubble corrects your eye. It is not deceived. It is always sincere. Put up a wall, and you think you're doing a great job, but the bubble in the spirit level may come along and tell you you're not, it's not straight, however much you think the opposite. And it's the bubble that's right.

The bubble in a spirit level, that drop of intelligent emptiness, has exercised a hypnotic attraction over my eye ever since. The immediate reflex of checking the level, or lack thereof, in the objects around it. Tools were the best toys we children had. The idea of making a boat wasn't an imaginary intention. We could give it a go – and we did. We had wood, we had tools. And the sea wasn't far away. An excess of nails brought about our failure on the first day. In the end, however, the problem was financial, not naval. If we wanted to go hunting for treasure in Castro, we had mattocks, pickaxes and shovels. And we went. It wasn't a joke. Torques had turned up together with a beautiful Celtic diadem with triskeles and a clasp in the shape of a golden duck, that emigrant from here to the beyond. The trouble was, as Pepe de Amaro explained to us on our return from digging, defeated, that it's not you who finds the treasures, it's the treasures that come looking for you. The truth is we children in Castro liked tools almost as much as football. Not to work with, of course, just to play at working.

Access to our house was not that easy. The water supply was a public fountain in the grounds of the vicarage, where there was also a place for washing. But the supply was intermittent, given the character of the parish priest, who was somewhat feudal, not to say Neolithic. So there was an important problem. My father went searching for an essential treasure: water. The house was on a hillside, and he dug a well, convinced a spring would soon appear. He dug and dug. He came across granite and fought bravely against the stone with a mallet, iron wedges and even dynamite. It was unbelievable: there was water everywhere except in that well. While he went exploring in different parts of the property, the water would rise to the surface on the floor of our house, in the most hidden corner, under the beds, with effervescent irony. The house was located under a kind of atmospheric passage in the north-west of the peninsula, which is where the most powerful formations of Atlantic clouds came in. This wasn't a subjective impression. It was what the Weatherman said, with his Stick in the Atmosphere.

The first time I met the figure of the Weatherman was when we were able to watch television in Leonor's pub. This Mariano Medina – that was his name – seemed like a nice enough guy, I have no doubt. All the customers, who normally ignored the news, would be all ears whenever Medina appeared, his sobriety emphasised by thick glasses and the stick for indicating isobars. The weather maps back then were not in colour. Everything was either black or white. After a short discussion about high and low pressure, the pointer would invariably gravitate, with inclement insistence, towards Castro de Elviña and, more specifically, towards the roof of our house, in order to announce the approach of the Azores cyclone. This atmospheric phenomenon, with its boxer's name, was always punctual. It would unleash seas of water that flooded everything – except for the well my father was digging.

Spring arrived. The Weatherman withdrew his pointer for several days, and a better job turned up. My father was asked to build a small house for some neighbours, the Baleiros, a family who had emigrated to the north of England. When he returned to his work, next to the emergent Baleiro home, my father drew a circle early one morning and set about digging. First, with a hoe. It was black earth, good earth, that let itself be sifted. There then appeared a layer of muddy sand mixed with stones. It stuck to the pickaxe and was heavier to shovel. The day was sunny, and my father dug down with happy excitement, convinced that this time he wouldn't be beaten by the void. It smelled of water. He could hear the murmurs. At dusk, the spring was already licking his boots. By nightfall, he came out of the well with festive splashing, water around his ankles. The well, on that first day, must have been about two metres, a little above his head.

It hurt him, the way the well dried up. The way the spring made fun of him. One day, he brought along a water diviner. He called him 'Mister Dowser'. The old man seemed very professional. He scoured the hillside with a thin stick that seemed to emerge from his fibrous hands like a strange eleventh finger he could roll and unroll. At one point, he stopped. He lowered his head, like someone hearing the first whimper of water, and the stick appeared to move, almost vibrating. But it was only a passing shiver. He repeated the operation with a pendulum, a chain from which he hung a cylindrical object with a conical point like a bullet. Nothing. It didn't move anywhere in the garden. That stupid pendulum might have moved inside the house. The old man didn't want to be paid. He really was a gentleman. There was a hydric sadness in his eyes. The spring remained silent, hiding somewhere. My father's face stiffened that evening when the Weatherman appeared on the television in Leonor's pub, with his infallible stick. The pointer, again, directly over our house.

10

The Celtic Treasure
and the Astronaut

In restless paradise, we lived from one day to the next, but also in history. In the school account, history mimicked the flight of a bird of prey over the Castro henhouses. It turned up suddenly, as if it had come not from another place on earth, but from a forest rooted in the clouds. It then went into a helicoidal flight, a succession of perfect curves, until accurately pouncing with its claws on the target. The present – that was its prey. In the accounts of the low voices, the movement of history resembled the flight of a bat. There's a bat that still flies on the dark side of my memory. Somebody found it in a granary, where it was sleeping its long winter sleep, hanging from a beam. We woke it up. We seized it by the tips of its wings. We tried to make it fly by throwing it against the light of a street lamp. The bat sluggishly moved its wings, tried to escape the nightmare, but fell down again. In the first act of unkindness, we found something comical about its face, with its human features. Until we became aware of the amazement in its blind look. Animals help us see. If there's a flight I find fascinating, it is the flight of bats. It was a gift of guilt. The complete disarray, the unexpected twists and turns, the disruption of perspective, being visible and invisible at the same time. A total irony of the senses. Hallucinatory present.

Unlike the historical chronology of school lessons, its heavy-machinery, unperturbed advance, in the accounts of the low voices tenses and episodes got mixed up. In appearance. As in the flight of a bat. As in the cubist print of a carnival. Near the ruins of the ancient indigenous settlement, on the best lands in Elviña Valley, expropriated by means of intimidation, they stuck a powerful factory for chemical fertilisers, Cross Fertiberia. The fruit trees soon fell ill, and the birds that used to alight on them disappeared. The Roman expedition by sea to quell the Artabrian rebels, the first Viking attack on the peninsula, the Battle of Elviña in 1809, the barbarities of 1936, all formed a succession of crazy acts that got mixed up in time. The large rock where Sir John Moore had his control post and was mortally wounded is popularly known as the Crag of Goliacho. Ana Filgueiras searched every nook and cranny in Castro for the root of this name. She wondered why it had to be Goliacho. And an old man replied with biblical precision, 'That comes from the time David defeated Goliacho.' Now, in the hallucinatory present, the contaminative factory had arrived. The wind scattered pollen, but also a futuristic plague. We grew up surrounded by an optimism about progress. When we came out of school, at midday, a plane would pass overhead on its way to Alvedro Airport, and we would greet it enthusiastically, running along, waving our arms about and shouting in the hope we might make ourselves heard, 'Sweets, sweets!' Some old people would mutter under their breath, 'Beetles, more like. That's what they're going to throw down. Beetles!' In summer, we would sometimes go down to Santa Cristina Beach, a merry band of boys and girls singing, 'Tourist one million nine hundred and ninety-nine thousand nine hundred and ninety-nine!' And old Pego, who used to graze a tiny flock of depressed sheep, would murmur, 'The winter will be here soon enough!'

But there were still treasures to be found. Going in search of treasure didn't seem such a stupid idea. If an old woman told us there was a golden beam from Os Curutos to O Lagar, for us children this wasn't a story, but a piece of confidential information. The question was how to get hold of it. On the hill, Os Curutos, were the ruins of the city that put up a fight against the Romans. The teacher told us one day, in a serious voice, that we owed everything to the Roman Empire. But who were these earlier builders? They had an obsession with circles. They made circular houses with circular forts. Could they communicate? They probably said, 'Boh!' The ruins were fairly complete. A thick cobweb of undergrowth covered the three circular walls, the labyrinthine alleys and the mysterious cistern of the ancient settlement. They carried out an archaeological dig there from 1947 to 1952, and discovered the treasure of Castro de Elviña, which is kept in the museum of St Anthony's Castle. It is said to have belonged to a priestess. One of the objects is the diadem with a clasp in the shape of a bird, a wonder of Celtic craftsmanship. I've often gazed long and hard at this golden palmiped. It seems to swim in the symmetry of ornate curves. It's funny. The finest artistic heritage from our ancient Galician past is two feminine objects: the Castro diadem and the Caldas de Reis comb. Apparently, very few weapons turned up during the excavations. Who knows what significance this holds?

So there we were, playing at hunting for treasure. Calmly. Most of all in Castro, but also in A Casa Vella and the woods of A Zapateira, where Soult's French troops and Moore's light infantry of Highlanders engaged. We carried farming implements and dug like that crazy Schliemann in search of Troy. That was all the metal we ever found – other rusty implements. Iron came face to face with its own ghost. The most extraordinary discoveries were the skeleton of a bike, a few cans of beer and some prehistoric condoms. But the treasure was there. We could feel the presence of the golden duck. We really could. Though what we heard was the constant hum, like a warning, of the high-voltage tower they decided in the years after the war to plant right on the *ara solis* of the most important *castro* along this coast. We were children playing, and yet, without knowing anything of history, we knew there was an element of symbolic fatality, of humiliation, in the brutal fact of having stuck the tower in the heart of this ancient settlement. To warn of the risk, there was a sign with a drawing that showed a little man being zapped by a bolt of lightning. The electric hum inside our heads was very strong. Whenever a storm drew near, the sound would transmute into a grinding of teeth. There is a continual debate going on in Galicia as to whether the Celts were here or not. Not long ago, on the Portal Galego da Língua website, the debate about a Celtic presence was reignited due to an article by Fermín Bouza. Sparks were flying off the Internet. I had to exercise a great deal of self-control not to send a piece of confidential information that emanated from my childhood, which the others knew nothing about: 'Stop scratching your heads. Stop turning the question around. The Galician Celts all died of electrocution!'

Another historical place was A Casa Vella – also known as the Frenchman's House – the ruins of an old ecclesiastical building that was badly affected by the cruelty of the Napoleonic battle on 16 January 1809. More or less around that date, in the same place, but in our times, the historical effect of the bat's flight led to warlike skirmishes between the young people of Palavea-Cyprus and Castro. They were the ones who attacked, since they were more urban. The Castro lot took up defensive positions in the ruins, as always. There were people dressed up as Indians, cowboys, Romans, and even the odd Mexican in a mariachi hat. Whether we were Celtic or not, we clearly originated from the Far West, including those from Cyprus. A historical mix-up that normally ended up in a game of football, that more sophisticated form of war that requires the ideas to reach your feet.

One of our local heroes was Ramón (Moncho) Tasende, who would become Spanish 5000-metre champion, but back then competed epically in cross-country races. And, before that, in cycling. He ran like an Ethiopian. His younger sister, Maruxa Tasende, was of the same stock. She was a great athlete, a long-distance runner. But the first time we saw her in action was with the women's football team during carnival. The world was upside down. Never again did I see someone run and dribble down the wing as she did.

Moncho Tasende never drank wine or beer, only Mirinda soft drinks or something like that, but the greatest spectacle, which we followed enviously, was watching him eat mounds of monkey nuts. He would pile them up into a pyramid on top of one of the barrels in Leonor's pub. 'It's because of the fibre!' he used to explain. And he was right. If one really were a writer, this is the menu one would have. Because what literature wants is fibre for cross-country running. In Castro, you had to be quick when it came to being born or dying. Even when deceased, you had to walk, since the cemetery was miles away, alongside St Vincent's Church. There was a dirt track to Elviña – that was, until man landed on the moon, since it was just before the Apollo 11 landing in the summer of 1969 that the track got tarmacked. There was a lot of talk about astronauts back then, and the man who operated the tar gun, moving about Castro in a white suit with floating steps over the gravel, certainly looked as if he'd just come from a NASA space mission. Until he took off his helmet. It was very hot, something that was worsened by the sweating of the asphalt. His face was covered in the gelatinous glue of a jellyfish. Someone ran to offer him a jug of water. It took him a while to speak as he caught his breath, the words melting on his lips. Our astronaut finally explained that he'd been sent by the county council. And the work, for what it was, was not particularly well paid.

11

The Weight of the
World on Their Heads

She carries a shape that is about her size, but gives the impression it's heavier than she is. It's not just any old shape. The washerwoman's bundle is a perfect sphere. Resting on her head. Sometimes, there are several of them, in a caravan. Like the women carrying conical pyramids of a hundred lettuces each in their baskets.

The topography of paths was largely a construction of women carrying essential things on their heads. In Castro de Elviña, old roads came together, like 'The Mountaineers', an old royal road, and cart tracks with names that evoked not just a destiny, but a way of walking. 'Apparition', for example, along which walked the living and the dead. 'Goblin'. These deep pathways formed part of a loom on which the walker's shuttle wove the known and unknown that could take you anywhere in Galicia. In addition to the main routes, throughout the whole territory, hill and dale, there was a palimpsest of writing on the ground, cryptic in appearance, but which always led to a place-in-waiting. My mother tells me, 'Follow the path of the broody hen.' And they really existed. The hen. The path. The nest. Or the road to Perfecto's mill. That also existed. The mill. And Perfecto.

My favourite was the overgrown road. The track to A Cavaxe. The old path that came from Mesoiro Valley and skirted the fort in Castro. Each path has its own imagination. Paths die whenever they stop telling stories. This path I'm talking about was overgrown for much of the year. It had fallen into disuse. Besides, we lived a long way from there, over on the other side. And yet my sight became entangled in it. I remember one day in winter, it was raining and a funeral procession appeared around the bend. This scene taken out of a film wasn't entirely without reason. Mesoiro and Feáns belonged to the parish of St Vincent of Elviña, and they would often come on foot to bury their dead, bearing the coffin on their shoulders for several miles. The overgrown path opened that day to reveal the extreme gait of sadness. Moving in heavy, congested order, the black umbrellas raised like tarred shields against the leaden sky, the funeral procession advanced. What they were carrying was a small, white coffin. Whenever a child died, it was an angel dying. But I had the impression that day, I don't know why, that God himself had died. Had got smaller. Had curled up inside a bluish-white coffin under the storm.

I felt great respect towards that path to A Cavaxe. The way it opened and closed. It opened again, and there was the disturbing vision of some young lads from the other side of Orro, carrying a hunted wolf tied to a stretcher, the ghost of a wolfless wolf, a hide that death itself had abandoned. It may have been the last wolf, and they were the last wolf men. Even in the way they asked for coins, they demonstrated a lack of enthusiasm.

One day, on the path to A Cavaxe, some acrobats turned up. It was around the time the Price Circus came to A Coruña, pulling in the crowds, with Pinito del Oro on the trapeze. But this small group of circus performers used to do the rounds of villages and suburbs. I don't remember what they were called – we used to call them the Saltimbancos, which wasn't a bad name. Their main acts were the Wise Donkey, the Invincible Man and the acrobatics of the Flying Girl. They performed two nights in Castro, in a field belonging to Felipe, a farmer who once paid us five pesetas for helping with the threshing and gave us the money in such a way that we wore it like a medal. Which just goes to show how important the manner of giving is. People really enjoyed the number with the donkey and the strongman, and other distractions, but not nearly so much as the acrobatic girl, who, as soon as she appeared on stage, with what for me was a death-defying leap, formed part of the Enigmatic Organisation of the Unforgettable. She was just a girl, but she grew before our very eyes. We watched her grow. She had very long hair gathered in a ponytail. This also responded to one of the senses. The final act was the Flying Girl. She climbed up onto the shoulders of the Invincible Man, tied a tall metal platform to him with a harness and, attaching her ponytail to the top of the pinnacle, gave herself a push and started turning and turning in the night. Without support, with only the mooring of her hair. There is, in the Enigmatic Organisation of the Unforgettable, a second image of the Flying Girl. It's the following day, next to the Laranxeiro river, the washerwomen's favourite. The Flying Girl is in a bathing suit. Washing her hair very slowly. She lies down in the sun, on the grass. Her hair covers half the field. What a lovely surprise for the grass.

On Sundays, along the path to A Cavaxe, there appeared horses with riders dressed as mariachis. No, they hadn't just come off a television or film set in order to start walking. Groups of Mexican musicians were famous back then. They would come down from the mountains in Galicia as if they'd just arrived from

Washerwomen by the Laranxeiro river

Jalisco. Not anymore. The one arriving now is not on horseback.
He's a cyclist with his bike over his shoulder. I have always
admired people who carry their bikes, rather than the other way
round. In Castro, there were several such cyclists I hardly ever
saw riding their bikes. They never pushed their bikes very hard.
They would delicately place a hand on the handlebars, and in
this way the two of them would lead each other along. A high
degree of civilisation.

Is that the undergrowth opening? Who's coming along the
path now? It's another cyclist. This one is riding his bike. He's
certainly pedalling. His name is Maxi. He has a large roll on his
back, and a brush with a handle, a kind of strange mast. Hanging
on the handlebars is a bucket. He's bringing the cinema posters.
The closest ones to us are Portazgo Cinema in Burgo Estuary and
Monelos Cinema at the city gates. He's going to stick them to the
billboard that hangs on the large wall of the Cardama estate, with

its palm tree where all the sparrows from Elviña Valley congregate once a day. I always stop to have a look at the cinema posters and the palm tree. Only when the starlings arrive is it possible to see so many birds together. The palm tree tweets, chirps, chatters, warbles. It must be going mad with so many birds on its head.

Who's that descending the path on a motorbike? In a helmet, he looks as if he's concentrating hard, his body in a dynamic posture, close to the machine. It's Rafael the cobbler. When he gets off, you can see he's short and has a hump. This is not exactly the place to start, but he doesn't mind, he spreads luck wherever he goes, all you have to do is see him. Some people are even jealous. What wouldn't they give to have a hump like the cobbler's! I like to take our family's shoes to be repaired in his workshop in Elviña on a Saturday afternoon. Every Saturday afternoon, if at all possible. The workshop is small. You arrive, sit down on a stool. He is opposite, behind his worktable, in his leather apron. His head is big, enormous, with an impish grin. The whole ceiling is covered in images of naked or almost naked bodies, photos, calendars, posters, cut-outs from foreign magazines: a cosmopolitan collage, an infinite and fertile erotic landscape.

'You can come back for the shoes later.'

'No, no. I prefer to wait.'

My eyes always gravitate towards the same model, the same calendar. He follows the direction of my gaze.

'She never gets a year older!'

I am about to reach the curve in the road that leads from Elviña to Castro. After a long straight stretch, there's an abrupt ninety-degree turn. There were days the wind, coming back from school, wouldn't let us walk. We played with it, and it had fun. Clinging to each other's arms, we stood against it, and the wind pushed us back, as they say master stonemasons do to move stones by pushing them with their fingertips. A touch more, and we'd take to the air like kites. Where are the Castro children? The wind has taken them! That bend in the road was the best place to keep an eye on the track to A Cavaxe. It must have been a little windy because the undergrowth swayed when the path opened to make way for the Unforgettable. Out of the vegetal tunnel emerged Blondie of Vilarrodrís in her captain's uniform.

We'd seen the odd match on Shrove Tuesday between single and married ladies, all of them local. They would play on a pitch next to the Avenue that belonged to the bar Parada, which was where the Cockroach and other buses stopped. It was such a modest, stony pitch that all teams gave themselves a chance of winning. Lightning Football Club then built a new stadium, complete with changing rooms, and at carnival it was decided to celebrate this fact with an *international* match. Here comes Blondie with her team from the adjoining parish, Arteixo.

Running across country, for miles, in a football shirt and shorts. All of this, as the poet Manuel María wrote, in those 'incestuous times'. At the front, like a model in a Pirelli calendar, like an optical revolution in that era of textile mourning, was Blondie of Vilarrodrís. She had emigrated and, on her return, opened a bar called Odette. She wore her hair in the flapper style and bore a certain resemblance to Brigitte Bardot. Not that the two needed comparing. Blondie of Vilarrodrís was there. She was real. So much so that she'd just jumped through the bracken in order to pass from the invisible to the visible along the track to A Cavaxe. Now, on the football pitch, she demonstrated her silky skills. And, something that was a little more complicated, she graciously turned to face the roaring crowd, which had come from all around and was emitting *arias di bravura* every time the girls of Elviña, Castro and Vilarrodrís touched the sphere of the world.

On Shrove Tuesday, there was always someone to block the streams so the rivers would dry up and the washerwomen wouldn't have to go to work and could come and play, or at least watch, those games that marked a turning point in women's football. The carnival mandate was fulfilled: it was necessary to turn the world upside down!

What happened during the rest of the year was the exact opposite. The washerwomen of Castro de Elviña carried the sphere on top of their heads. They washed for upper-class families in A Coruña or for clinics, hotels, restaurants. They came and went with enormous loads balanced on a crown or pad, most of the time on foot, sometimes with a donkey. In the caravan, there were also women who sold fresh produce in the city squares. It was noticeable, the way they carried their merchandise. A form of aesthetics developed by the imagination of necessity. An earthen algebra: the positioning kept the fruit alive. It was possible to meet the fishwife along the track. Almost always, whenever she got to our house, all she had left was horse mackerel. I hated them. Children simply don't like fish bones, and that's all there is to it. But there was one day the fishwife, coming up the hill, struck me as the most extraordinary creature in existence. She was carrying a basket full of sea urchins.

Women came and went with weights on top of their heads in order to have their hands free to carry other heavy things or the weight of a child. Everything they carried was necessary. Essential. Provisions, water, milk, wood. Clothes. Some washerwomen's hands were worn down by soda. Their backbones, because of the weights they carried, looked like inverted pyramids. It was amphibian work, always in contact with water, with a damp stone, feeling the cold. Talking of visions on the road, I once saw the washerwomen of Castro with the sphere of the world on their heads. What happened every Shrove Tuesday was that they and other workers would kick the male's planetary ball around. Their shrieks of laughter resound in the empty stadiums, race over the grass, like a triumph of humanity.

12

Drinking the Rainbow

The city knew little or nothing about Castro. Those from Castro, apart from knowing about the city, had a universe of their own. A gift of knowledge. Atmospheric, for example. From when we were children, we received a thorough meteorological education. In modern times, they stuck the university in that area, but there already existed a popular School of Winds, Storms and Clouds. One of the first things my new friends in Castro taught me was how to catch a rainbow with my hands. There were puddles where the rainbow would place its artistic desire with oily density. You could feel the spectrum of all the colours of the cosmos in your hands. Lift them to your mouth. Lick, taste, drink the rainbow.

It was no accident that the football team, founded when people stole the ball from the elites and discovered how to play in the mud, should be given and still bears the name Elviña Lightning. Seen from Castro, the bolts of lightning were nightmares from the open sea: sudden, fierce, incandescent forests that seized the celestial void with anxiety and rage. There was a wonderful rock from which to watch the natural cinema of lightning. The Cuckoo's Crag, near our house, on the way to O Escorial. The cuckoo was large, sculpted by the weather's imagination in the free workshop of the elements. Any sculptor would have immediately gone down in history for a work like that. It looked like a bird, with its stone wings, its golden-green lichen eyes and its beak pointing towards the city, in axial connection with the Tower of Hercules-Breogán.

We would climb and sit on the cuckoo's neck, feel the excitement of those who have always dreamed of flying. There was a sweeping panorama of the whole Artabrian bay. The call of the West. There, like an invisible nation, was the Compass Rose. Many years later, after my military service, I found out that heavy machinery had demolished the Cuckoo's Crag. I never thought the death of a stone could hurt so much.

From that prominence and other lookouts, we could see a storm approaching A Coruña long before anybody in the city knew about it. During rainy spells, the washerwomen would spread out their clothes whenever it cleared. That time of light between downpours, like the pause between the ticking of a clock.

When water was sighted by the Tower, the Castro washerwomen knew they had three emergency minutes. A succession of alarm calls would ring out. They would cover and uncover the clothes horse of the mountain and fields. Memory retrieves these images like the activism of an artistic will. This is what it was. Same as the pyramids of a hundred lettuces! The tied lettuces were jewels in the fields of Castro and Elviña Valley. They sealed them with bulrushes so they would swell on the inside and, having cut them, the women would take them to sell in the squares of A Coruña. They carried them in baskets. Each basket, a hundred lettuces. No more, no less. They placed them in concentric circles to form a conical construction that was crowned by the hundredth lettuce. Everything the women carried on their heads was essential. I can see the women with pails of water. The women with pitchers of milk. The women with bundles of clothes. The women with bales of hay. The fishwives with their wares. Since there's nothing else I can do, I would like to place inside Miss Celia's basket or bucket a verse from Nelly Sachs's 'Epitaphs Written in the Air': 'Irradiated by fish in a glorious dress of tears.'

In Castro, a sister and brother were born, Sabela and Francisco Xavier, known as Chavela and Paco. There was one day my mother said, 'Sit over there and hold out your arms.' So I sat opposite her, and my arms became the support for unravelling or making a skein of wool. Ever since that day, hours of silence have had a sound. A precise, laborious percussion. A textile music. That of knitting. Enigmatic articles would materialise, in keeping with a miniature human anatomy. The first thing my mother knitted was a pair of woollen socks. As she finished these doll-sized booties, my mother was sending a message, like someone waving two flags in the International Code of Signals: 'Something new is about to be born!'

My mother always took great care that our feet were warm. She waged a relentless war against the cold, damp and draughts. Children were always frightened of the wolf or the Sack Man, but for my mother the worst monsters of all were the Drip Man or the Man with Draughts. These poor monsters loved us a lot. They always kept us company, whether they were visible or not. They formed part of our home. As did the Weatherman. He may never have realised this. He must have had his own life. Drawn his maps every day. Careful with the Azores. Here's a patch of low pressure. There's a high. Without preference. He never showed much enthusiasm for one or the other. His stick was the stick of destiny, and he provided the voice. He looked like someone you could trust, but without influence. His stick had a life of its own. It decided. Pointed at our roofs, our heads, and kept returning to Castro de Elviña.

At home, before gas became the norm, we had an iron stove, the so-called *bilbaína* or *económica*. This is where my mother would hold a drying camp every winter. My father came back one evening looking as if he'd just survived a shipwreck. He'd first got wet on site and then become soaked on his journey home on the Lambretta. This was an elastic motorbike that accommodated four of us. How? With a desire for style in the way we were positioned. The fact is my father turned up, looking pale and miserable. As he shakily changed into something dry, my mother spread the wet clothes that were stiff with mud, like a diving suit, over the iron stove. I was by the stove as well, doing my homework in the warmest place. And that was when my mother paused in what she was doing, became aware of my presence and, staring at me, said in an almost reproachful tone:

'When you grow up, I hope you find yourself a job where you don't get wet!'

13

Franco's First Funeral

The chestnut tree in Souto had chestnuts for all the world.

The chestnut tree, when it was young, was painted by the great Germán Taibo (A Coruña, 1889 – Paris, 1919) in his landscape *Souto de Elviña*. He must have seen something special in it, that genius of the eye who was too quickly taken by the Grim Reaper, along with the members of the Ailing Generation. Taibo was also the author of the most famous nude in Galician art, which showed his French lover, Simone Nafleux.

This marvel of creation can be seen in the town hall in A Coruña. During the dictatorship, the naked woman's picture was kept for a long time in a municipal basement, and even after it resurfaced, it would still be concealed whenever there was a public event or a visit by the authorities. When Archbishop Quiroga Palacios first came, they decided to cover the sensual work of art with a flowery cloth of red and white carnations. In the middle of the act, however, a draught came in and blew the cloth onto the floor. In front of the perplexed faces appeared the luxuriant body of the stunning Simone, with her golden locks. Archbishop Quiroga, who shared a peasant background, humour and bonhomie with his contemporary Pope John XXIII, went and exclaimed with roguish irony, 'But why on earth have you kept such a divine creature hidden?'

The chestnut tree was divine as well. There were other chestnut trees, but the one in Souto, very near the archaeological remains, next to the stream in O Lagar, was a biblical tree and a little bit communist, since it would multiply its chestnuts according to need. All you had to do was have a grain of faith. There was the day it looked a little exhausted, some beating it, others scurrying along its branches like squirrels, but if you trusted it, if you were patient, the chestnut tree would come up with a number of chestnuts for your necklace. Nobody left that place without enough conkers to make a necklace for All Souls. There was no boy or girl without that protective and edible ornamental rosary whose beads were cooked chestnuts.

They tasted better if you boiled them with catmint, a medicinal, aromatic herb we found by the sides of the road to O Escorial. The knowledge of herbs and plants was another thing we never learned at school. One day, my mother took me out for a strange harvest: to collect gorse flowers. Among the prickles, in the brambles, we pecked at blackberries like birds. But what was the point of collecting gorse flowers? It would be years before I heard that Breton legend which tells of how God wanted to create the most beautiful flower and started painting gorse flowers on a stick, in that yellow later recreated by Van Gogh. The trouble was, the devil was lurking about, and as soon as God left, he went and painted on the spines. So it was that gorse was born, the most striking symbol of this life of ours, the lineage's coat of arms: flower and thorn.

There we were on the mountain, harvesters of gorse flowers, filling a cloth bag held by my mother. Her serious face, the melancholic gleam of her eyes as she collected the flowers, constituted a last hope. We found this out when she said, 'They're for Aunt Maruxa, who's very ill. Gorse flowers are good for the heart.'

During All Souls in Castro, we made skulls by hollowing out pumpkins. At night, in the corners and on the darkest roads, they would shine with candles inside. To begin with, this custom filled me with fear. It seemed to come from a macabre place. But actually it was quite the opposite. A game that was both training and memory. Walking and running along the border between this world and the next. Sharing the parish of the living and the dead. In the parish of St Vincent, the gravedigger towards the end of the twentieth century was an exceptional man. He was from Castro and was known as Antonio O Chibirico. Our gravedigger was the life and soul of the party. A wonderful dancer. A funny, witty man whose imagination belonged to another time and whose humour was not always well understood. On occasion, he would approach the doors of taverns and shout, 'You have to keep on dying! You won't let a man earn a few pesetas!'

The normal thing is not to be 'normal'. The normal thing is to be different. This is what life teaches you when it remembers. There is Farruco, with all the shoes of a lifetime. He wasn't rich. He worked as a bricklayer's mate. But he kept everything. Recycled everything. If Castro was as clean as a new pin, it was because Farruco had passed by. He built himself an alternative architecture. A shanty-town architecture. He died, but part of it is still left because it was so well made and coated with naval paint from unfinished pots he collected. So the shanty town had the aesthetics of arks marooned on the mountainside. Though, for me, the greatest spectacle was seeing that row of shoes on a Sunday, from childhood to old age, and the way he polished each pair. There were the soles and heels of the years of life, like the rings in the trunk of the chestnut tree in Souto.

Apart from skulls made out of pumpkins, during All Souls

Antonio and the captain of the women's football team during carnival

children were given chestnuts and the odd sweet. When, years later, Halloween was imported with all its commercial fanfare, I remembered that chestnut tree in Souto, the gravedigger and socialite Antonio, and the carnival troupes. The Murmurers from Elviña. The Skulls from Castro. Sometimes, they would meet up along the way and become the Murmuring Skulls. The Mariner produced a wonderful *meco*, an effigy that had to be buried. A figure that was well endowed. With an enormous penis, sometimes made of wood. Other times, it was a real turnip taken out of the ground, of portentous size. They once stuck some photos of the tyrant to the effigy and accompanied it on the back of donkeys like Franco's Moorish Guard. The Priest would lead the way with a censer (this was the libertarian Pepe de Amaro, unless I'm much mistaken). The Pagan was also good at acting out the role of God's provisional minister. Needless to say, the Widow was a man. In between sobs, (s)he would recite the surrealist litany:

> *In saecula saeculorum*
> *pig meat bacon is.*

At which point, they would chuck the tyrannical effigy into the Monelos river.

They never hurt anybody. But despots don't have a sense of humour. The members of the troupes were arrested. Mistreated. Some remained in custody. Lent arrived with a sniff of fear. Caused not exactly by the pumpkins or the deceased.

14

The Teacher and the Boxer

We must both have been about six. It was my first day at school, and he came to meet me: Antonio, known as the Red. Reasonably enough. I noticed the flaming colour of his hair. The other children soon formed a ring around us. Yes, this was going to be the first day and the first fight. It had fallen to us. An older child placed a stick on Antonio's shoulder and then spurred me on, 'Let's see if you're a man and can take it off him!'

I don't recall at that moment having any particular interest in showing that I was a man. Given the situation I was in, I probably wouldn't have minded being taken for a more modest creature. But I realised there were times when one's fate has been written. It wasn't necessary to move. A shove launched me in the direction of the Red, the stick fell, and us with it, fighting, drawn by a fatal law of gravity. We later became friends. I remember one day, on our way to school, Antonio cheerfully informed me, 'I'm leaving for England tomorrow.'

He added, 'And you're staying here!'

He didn't say this to hurt me; it was just a statement of fact. He was right. But this annoyed me. There was always somebody emigrating. Why leave like this, one by one, and not all of us together?

On the subject of emigration, we always talk about the nostalgia of the one who leaves and not the one who stays at home. There is sadness in the one who is leaving, but also hope. The unmitigated sadness belongs to the one who isn't leaving. At that time, all emigration was to Europe, in particular Germany, England, Switzerland and France. But in Castro, as in the rest of Galicia, long before Marshall McLuhan, the theory and practice of the 'global village' was already well known. It was often to escape the hostile, suffocating atmosphere of local bosses, as evidenced by that song recovered by Xurxo Souto, which was sung when the large ocean liners departed for America: 'You're staying there, you're staying there, with priests, monks and soldiers!'

Castro was small, but it was a *mappa mundi*. If you asked around, you could hear news from the Dominican Republic, Cuba, Uruguay, Venezuela, California . . . Legendary names: Ventura, Cardama, O Trust, A Manca, Enrique de Bras, Evaristo da Ponte, Manolo of Africa, Manolo Martín . . . In our childhood, however, most had a European destination. And, if it was sad to leave, the return of the 'emigrant's suitcase' was a cause for celebration. An ark containing wonderful new things. For us, not just toys you couldn't get here, but also, during adolescence, the smugglings of desire: records, magazines with naked bodies, daring clothes . . .

The first television set I ever saw, before Leonor's pub had one, was that brought by Rigal and Sara when they returned from Germany. They were among the first emigrants to Germany and returned in the early 1960s. When their television set was installed, the house was taken over by the local neighbourhood. The picture wasn't very good, but it didn't matter. Standing next to the screen was María Vitoria, Rigal and Sara's daughter. She also had come back from Germany! Blonde with pigtails, tall, a mysterious look. Actually, perhaps we were the mysterious ones, the way we gawped at her. But why look at the screen if you could look at María Vitoria?

In Castro, the first teacher I had was called Don Bartolo. Everybody there had a nickname, and his was White Horse. That was the first thing I learned, before I even got into the classroom. The state school was called Catechism, which just goes to show the ironic precision of the locals when it comes to naming things. The teacher was a stocky man who cast a shadow of doctrine and fear. On the far wall, behind the teacher's desk, the school was presided over by a crucifix and a large portrait of the dictator with an ermine robe and a rider's whip. They hung there, the two of them, but in very different conditions. Jesus on the cross, naked, nailed, with the crown of thorns and clotted blood on his head and back. Franco the emperor, lofty gaze, larger than his stature, with the powerful presence that comes from being well clothed. Three years with the same stage set in front of our eyes was a long time. The eyes send information, and then the imagination starts working on its own. What you could see was the Caudillo who ruled over everything and everyone, and that helpless, abandoned King of Kings who'd been beaten to death. Christ was a little higher, his head tilting towards the right. The Crucified's gaze indicated the man with the whip. He clearly had something to do with it.

At school, a great deal of importance was given to the so-called Formation of the National Spirit. The teacher was a man who was confident in what he was saying. It couldn't be otherwise. Sometimes, he took us into the playground, an open area separated from the mountain and fields only by a hedgerow, made us each pick up a stick and, in a martial voice, directed manoeuvres to confront the enemy. The enemy existed. Anti-Spain existed. We weren't quite sure what it was, what it looked like, but it existed and he would sometimes give it a name: the Red Hordes, the Judaeo-Masonic Conspiracy, Perfidious Albion. Denominations that were reminiscent of the youth gangs active in areas of cheap housing, which were known as Cyprus or Korea. In any case, for us, this was a bit of fun. Crawling along the ground, camouflaged by the grass, joyfully obeying the order to shoot anything that moved: crows, sheep, the jet aircraft that left behind two vapour trails in the sky because of our firepower. We played our war games in a place that had once been a battlefield. The scene of the Battle of Elviña. One of our forts was precisely the large rock, the Crag of Goliacho, where the Napoleonic French mortally wounded Sir John Moore. While working the land, my father came across a button that said *Liberté, Égalité, Fraternité*. There was a hiding place in the rock where Moore was cut down, with a vegetal covering of laurels. Here we smoked our first cigarettes, which were sold individually at the exit to Monelos Cinema. Here we trembled in another war. The war of first embraces. Furtive love.

The teacher had a stick he used as a pointer for the blackboard and maps. But sometimes, when the man became consumed by anger, the stick would turn into a primitive, terrible weapon. I remember the day he laid into one of the boys, Rafael, who was a little younger than me. The boy suddenly wriggled free, let rip a fearful howl and legged it out of the classroom. At this point, the teacher, with his staff of office, announced, 'After him! And, when you've got him, bring him back here!'

So it was we went after Rafael like a pack of hounds. He was lucky he was as fleet-footed as a hare. But our pursuit was relentless, following the master's orders. I understood that day there is no greater pleasure for a human than hunting down another human. But something unexpected happened. When we were far away from the school and the teacher could no longer see us, a dissident emerged from the pack of pursuers, stretched out his arms and stopped us. It was Xoán, the giant of the school. He had previously broken a leg. He'd fallen off a wall, and a rock had landed on top of him. He went to hospital and, when he came back, he was twice as big. Apparently, they'd tried out a vitamin complex on him. We all wanted to break a leg after that, so we could receive these extraordinary vitamins. But Xoán did not abuse his power. He was a good classmate. His fist now panned across our faces. And he said, 'Anyone who touches the boy will get a beating that will land him at the gates of hell!' Or something like that. A biblical mouth. A biblical fist as well. The feeling one had come face to face, in body and soul, with the beginning of all things.

The teacher in Elviña was called Don Antonio. He adored that black boxer, Cassius Clay, later renamed Muhammad Ali to remove the inherited trace of slavery. We used to study a list of Visigothic kings, the great deeds of the conquistadors of America, but, in our school around the middle of the 1960s, the real king was Cassius Clay. All because of the teacher. To stand up or walk, he needed crutches. His legs were short and he rotated as he walked, leaving sudden, anatomical wakes in the air behind him. An illness from his childhood, they said. Apart from that, he was a well-built man with the neck of a bull. When he sat in his chair behind the desk, his smooth, prominent head that looked as if it had been varnished, his graphitic look, which was dark and shiny, turned him into a kind of hypnotic, feared idol. Even the globe, positioned on his desk or on top of the wardrobe that served as a library and archive, resembled a minor satellite orbiting that human star. When he moved, the motive power – his energetic head – kept the motionless part of his body on tenterhooks and seemed to carry the fate of the whole class. He had the added misfortune of living on an upper floor in a house near the school, which left him no choice but to climb and descend twenty steps every day. He did this on his own, leaning on his crutches. This was his battle. A struggle we pupils witnessed every morning, the way he came down, twisting and turning, confronting the malfunctions of his body on the lethal arena of the staircase.

Don Antonio was a rapid man, mentally agile, with a gaze that encompassed the invisible. From his panoptic perspective, he could see the classroom upside down and inside out. He couldn't just read your thoughts. You could feel the trepanation,

Don Antonio's school in Elviña

the way he extracted your thoughts and dissected them on the desk. Why didn't he call out from the staircase? Why didn't he let someone help him? He would glance over at us from the landing, while we watched him out of the corner of our eyes. The vision of his slow descent was the image of an epic, painful story, of wounded knowledge. The laborious passage became a kind of sinister rite. Nobody would have been surprised if a trap-door had opened in the staircase one day and the teacher had disappeared.

In class, he was efficient and hard. He could even be cruel when it came to corporal punishment, the way he moved his strong arm and the stick acquired an autonomous existence, detached from the brilliant brain. I can see him now, or at least I think so. The teacher's perplexed gaze, the way he checks his own arm, having beaten a pupil. This used to happen a lot during catechism on a Saturday morning. Only the right answer would do. For some reason, he was always tense that day. We had to memorise everything, he never explained anything. He took the lesson, and there was no room for mistakes. Not even when it came to the episode with Balaam's donkey. The stick and the ruler were work implements. They weren't just taking up space. The first day of class, one boy would hand the teacher the instrument of punishment by order of his parents. Don Bartolo used it as much as Don Antonio. This wasn't a topic that was ever discussed outside of class. Or in class, either. Don Antonio was competent. The one who taught best. Though he did have a problem with women. Not just with one or two. With the female race. With all of them, or so it seemed. The worst insult for a child was to be called a 'little woman'. When he reached this limit, the tone of his voice would prick like a needle:

'Little woman! You're just like a little woman!'

Everything in him changed, speech and body, when a fight

in the world heavyweight boxing championship was due to be broadcast. That day, he would transfer our class to the bar O da Castela, which had the only television in that part of Elviña. As far as I know, a unique, unprecedented move in Spain and perhaps in the world. He didn't care what others might think. Cassius Clay versus Sonny Liston. The whole class in motion. And at the front, flying on Canadian crutches, a body making quick, abrupt strokes, in the direction of the ring, locked in combat with the world: the teacher.

15

You Will Never Be Abandoned

We children slept on folding beds. This way, in the morning, when we got up, our bedroom could become the sitting room. From that window, you could see the city like a large, illuminated ship, the friendly light of the lighthouse, which proclaimed in Morse code, 'You will never be abandoned!' To the west, there were other, frightening glows that emanated from the furnaces and chimneys of the oil refinery in Bens. They looked like giant flame-throwers, an apocalyptic picture in the night, since that was where the sun set. On the other side of the house, where the front door was, there was only mountain. A mountain with a split person-ality. During the day, the unending forest, the so-called Priest's Wood, was an undiscovered land for exploring, a place of adven-tures. At night, a hostile inferno, a place of loss, where the world's bad temper muttered and groaned.

One night, my father threw María and me out of the house. We must have been about nine. We used to fight a lot back then, like cat and dog. He wasn't in the habit of hitting. Nor was my mother. He would go to bed very early. For two reasons. Because at six he was already up, on his way to work. And because he didn't want to pay the electricity company any more than he had to. He wasn't a devotee of Our Lady of the Fist, but he was in permanent disagreement with the powers that ruled this world, be they the Vatican or Fuerzas Eléctricas del Noroeste. He had this intuition. Were we to follow his example, there would never be an energy crisis, nor would we suffer from climate change. He never gave way in his militancy against the electric empire. Even in his old age, when central heating was installed at home, he would silently go around turning off the radiators. When somebody complained about the temperature, he would keep quiet, like a member of the Secret Society of Disconnection. But back then we were reading like crazy and would await the arrival of the extinguisher of light with trepidation. He didn't put on a show. This was a stealth operation. He can't have enjoyed it, but the battle had to be won. We waited for a while. Until the sounds of sleep emerged from the master bedroom. Then we turned on the light. Like traitors.

But that wasn't the reason he threw us out of the house that night. He was right. He wanted to sleep, and we wouldn't stop fighting. That terrible bone of contention that can lead you to hate the person you love in a minute, and after that you don't remember what it was. We were struggling furiously when he got up, took us by the arm, opened the door and landed us beneath the stars, on the edge of that *locus horroris*, the Priest's Wood. We were amazed to hear the lock turning behind us. A minute earlier, we had hated each other and been scratching each other's faces. Now, suddenly, the two enemies were alone in the universe. Expelled from the hearth. And, as is well known, there is no greater fear than the fear of being abandoned.

We were alone in the night, listening to the inner sounds of the house, that solitary house of ours that resisted all tempests. How moved I was by the words Henri Bosco used to describe his home: 'The house fought bravely.' The truth is we soon stopped feeling the Hansel and Gretel syndrome. We forgot the cause of our fight. We held hands. We were more united than ever. We swore there would never be another war between us. And the spell worked. From a terrible sense of unease we went to a feeling of calm and then an exciting happiness. If the patriarchal door remained closed, where were we going to seek refuge?

There were our uncles and aunts. It is common these days to talk about the genome. The similarities and differences between humans and closely related animals such as chimpanzees, bonobos and orang-utans. It's not true that they don't have language or use tools. As the great Uruguayan Pablo Casacuberta once explained, we're almost identical in everything. What is the main difference? We humans have uncles and aunties!

And there María and I were, happily going through our wonderful list. A Gaiteira, O Birloque, Anceis, Sada, Sergude, the barber's shop on Bizkaia Street, the tavern in Almeiras . . . We even had an uncle in Seville: Benito, a meter reader for an electric company, as it so happened. I was under the impression Uncle Benito had walked from Corpo Santo to Seville as a young man, because I was always hearing about the way he walked. He wandered the streets of Seville on foot, from porch to porch, from meter to meter, and in summer the ground became scorching hot. Especially, one imagines, for an employee of an electric company whose job is to charge for kilowatts. Carmina's mother would always invite this nice young Galician, so well mannered, with a tenor's voice, into the courtyard, so he could rest in the shade and drink a lemonade. And that was how Benito and Carmina met and got married. Thanks to electricity. Quite apart from his opinion about companies in the electricity sector, my father, like everybody else, was very fond of Benito.

When he was much older, my father went to take the exam for his certificate of primary education. He studied a lot, with

107

my sister Sabela. He did everything well, but when they asked him the names of some parasites, he fell silent. He didn't want to say what he was really thinking. At the examiner's insistence, he gave the name of a parasite that had nothing to do with capitalism or politics: a tortoise. He was very pleased with himself for including this touch of irony. The examiner liked it as well. His next task was to write an essay.

The theme? 'My Holidays'.

My father put down his pen, stood up from the table and headed for the exit. The teacher called after him and asked for an explanation. Why leave now? He replied, 'I cannot write about something I do not know.' She kindly insisted, 'Please sit down. You may write about anything you like.' So my father wrote about Uncle Benito's adventure, the legend that he'd gone walking from Corpo Santo to Triana Bridge. He described this enchanting city where meter readers met luminous women in courtyards in the shade. They could even get married and be peacefully happy. And he added, 'I really liked Seville, I really did.' But he never went there. He didn't like long journeys. He liked travelling less and less. During his final years working, he would get up very early, two or three hours before he had to, and drive the Renault 4 or 'Cuatro Latas' very slowly, to avoid unfriendly traffic.

We had lots of places to go. Uncles and aunts formed a republic, in every sense of the word. There was Pepa in A Gaiteira, who'd always been a keeper of harmony. In O Birloque, Felicitas, but also Aunt Amparo with her sewing workshop. I loved going there. I have always felt well in hairdressing salons and sewing workshops. Half a dozen girls worked in Amparo's workshop and would laugh and gossip in time to the pedals of the sewing machines. Suddenly, the machines remained in suspense. The voice of Juana Ginzo or Matilde Conesa in the radio dramas of Guillermo Sautier Casaseca. That was how to reach the hearts of people. You had the right to stop your Singer out of emotion! A man, a little man, felt like a dandy in that place. Some of those girls must have been reading Corín Tellado. The equivalent for men was western novels. On this issue, I still had a few inches to grow. I was immersed in the comic books *Capitán Trueno* and *El Jabato*. The thing that would change everything, when I had my tonsils taken out, was reading *The Last of the Mohicans* in an illustrated edition by Bruguera. I now had my own hero, Uncas, with his turtle tattoo. A few inches later, the summer before starting at secondary, I took an overdose of the Far West. A kind of training. My friend from Castro, Manolo de Hilario, was a good supplier. And had good taste. He's still a great reader of the best literature. And a specialist in the installation of large cranes. Cranes, like ships, are the most fascinating human architecture. Railways as well. There we were, heading for the Far West. I trust his sense of smell, which had its beginnings in those discoveries he made when we were children. Most of the novels bore the signature of Marcial Lafuente Estefanía, but he would recommend other authors such as Keith Luger and Silver Kane. The style was different. Today, from time to time, there are still very serious fights between very serious writers on the subject of whether style exists or not, and what it is. I think these debates take place between people who have never read western novels with the necessary suspension of disbelief. On the hottest days in summer, when the hours were dozing in the shade, Manolo de Hilario and I were capable of reading five novels on the trot, and I swear the style – the aura even – was perfectly visible. The faces sent back reflections like a mirror. There was, for example, Silver Kane's smile. The oblique line of irony on his mouth. The electricity of erotic tension in his blazing eyes. Yes, the way Far West heterodoxy talked, when it achieved that mixture of sarcasm and irony, was something we felt very close. One of our local heroes was Juan Juanilla, the son of Corazón, an emigrant in Germany, who came back from the cold dressed as a card player on a Mississippi paddle steamer. He had that style. There were people who travelled long distances to watch him play *tute* in the bar. Not just because of his skill with the cards. For every trick, the right sentence. The fist banging down on the table. Here it comes: 'Ever since the invention of gunpowder, men have been finished!'

It was said people didn't even read one book per year, but the fact is they never took the chapbook into account. The one that sold for five pesetas and could even be rented from the kiosk. The girls had Corín Tellado. The truth is they read more than us. They were more avant-garde. In the hairdressing salons, there were gossip magazines and photo-novels. In the sewing work-shops, the fashion magazines were a joy to the eyes and the imagination in those sombre times. The models, who looked like aliens with their daring hairstyles and clothes, were the topic of conversation and much laughter. But they also somehow forced people to express an opinion. Liberality was measured in centi-metres. In little time, less than you might think, a girl would appear with the same hairstyle, the same clothes. On her own, walking down the road from Elviña to Castro, she could alter reality. Western novels could be read at any age. Years later, in the 1990s, I came across Silver Kane again. We were on the Irish Sea, having reached the 54th parallel, in the region of Black Rock, and he was being read in their bunks by iron sailors, real cowboys on that unceasing, indomitable frontier. Tied in so they wouldn't be knocked about by the waves, they read with an expression that was familiar to me. The oblique smile. Somebody reading out what the rich heiress of a ranch says to the guy who resists her: 'Listen, cowboy, I'm looking for a real man. Have you seen one anywhere?' Listen. The sailor reads aloud. It's Boquete from

Catoira who replies off the cuff, like a classic, 'There was one, girl; with you, that makes two of us.'

During that summer full of literature from the Far West, where was María? She really did keep to the frontier. We were palefaces, she was an Indian. At home, other, shabby-looking books started doing the rounds at night. One day, my mother opened one of those strange visitors, I remember it was *Hopscotch* by Julio Cortázar. She opened another, by Henry Miller. I can see her now, she read something that surprised her and then glanced at María: 'Don't go so fast!' My mother believed in the power of books. She loved them and feared them. She'd read lots of lives of saints.

My father heard us talking excitedly in the middle of our misadventure. Just like Uncle Francisco. He opened the door and sent us to bed without another word. María and I never fought again. And that night we still had time to turn on the light so we could read while my father fell down exhausted on the road to Seville.

16

A Family Photo

There is a family photo in the album. An official photo, so to speak. It was taken in a photo studio in Catro Camiños, in A Coruña. There are six of us – my parents and their four children, two girls and two boys. All looking very serious. In my parents, there is an expression of distrust. The camera, especially if it knows it's being questioned, registers that feeling very well. Still today, the photo contains a vibration of impatient hostility. Of course, it was possible for us all to pose happily together for a photo. There are photos like that, at a party, some time later. But if we're here, in the photo studio, it's out of a sense of duty, out of necessity. In order to apply for a university grant, something María and I wanted to do, we had to enclose a photograph that showed a 'numerous family'. I remember the day well. It was raining. My father had escaped from work and was in a hurry. He swept back his damp hair, which was a kind of time warp, in black and white.

The first family photo was taken several years earlier. One Sunday morning in summer. In Méndez Núñez Gardens, next to the monument dedicated to Concepción Arenal. A difficult place to forget, since the monument consists of a goldfish pond surrounded by thick chains, with the powerful presence of an iron eagle. It's a public holiday. Full of light. There must have been music and tastes, but they do not form an active part of my memory. The light does, though. Everybody carries a little light with them that day. My mother, for example, wears a hat with a tulle veil. She's the one who takes the initiative when the photographer appears. Yes, we'll have our photograph taken. Finally. My mother gathers us together. Tells us to pose. It's a shame we don't have a good portrait of the whole family. So it's not only an act of happiness, it's also a responsibility. An account that has to be settled with destiny. She positions us. Glances around. The final touch. That's it. Attention please!

Motionless. All of us looking towards the photographer. He's a fat man. Almost as wide as he is tall. He bears a certain resemblance to Oliver Hardy. He wipes his resinous brow with a handkerchief. He seems to be involved in a conflict with his body and clothes. A disaffected suit, too long or too short, who knows? He struggles with the knot in his tie. Stands up. Breathes. Stares. Examines, blinks, clicks his tongue. During the preparations, we remain very still, mute, with the complex of a group that doesn't fit. Eventually, he prepares the flash. Gestures with his left hand. Last warning. Looks through the viewfinder. Moves his right foot forward. Sways slightly, bends his knees. This position gives the man back a little symmetry.

'Smile!' he shouts. 'It's not a funeral!'

He jots down his address on the page of a notebook. He looks tall now. My mother searches in her bag for her purse. Opens it and takes out the money. These are two laborious, semi-secret operations. My father stands apart, his hands in his pockets. It's Sunday. The photo will be ready on Tuesday afternoon, no doubt about it. So there we are on Tuesday afternoon, accompanying my mother. No, my father is not part of the procession. He works as a builder all day. And sometimes as a musician at night. The address is in the area around Santa Lucía Market. We reach an alleyway. My mother checks the number on the piece of paper and knocks at the door. There is no answer. Nobody appears. She knocks louder. In the house opposite, an old woman opens the shutters on the first floor.

'Who are you looking for?'

'A photographer, madam! Is there not a photographer living here?'

The old woman closes the window with a mournful silence.

We went back another two or three times. But no. There was no photographer and nobody opened the window. On Sundays, my mother would carefully peruse the gardens. Pay attention to anybody with a camera. Yes, that one's fat. But people change, they have their right side and their wrong side. One day, she saw him – or thought she saw him – in the group next to the tombola. She ran after him. Cleared a way through the crowd. But the fat man had the speed of light. I sometimes think he's the one passing by when a man in a suit or overcoat suddenly overtakes me. Hefty, with long strides, fading out of sight. I imagine him going to his real home. Putting down the crippled camera. Opening a darkroom with all the golden memories of all the photographs he never took. There we are, smiling, as united as ever.

17

My Mother and the
Manifesto of Surrealism

Concentric circles were perhaps the first writing in Galicia, together with labyrinths and representations of deer. I say 'writing' because they are, without a doubt, signs telling a story in stone, a flint burin in the granite notebook at the mercy of the elements. Astral calendars, liturgical symbols, maps or primitive censuses? There they are, a circular psyche, a cyclical look interweaving time and timelessness. They're good for thinking and imagining, these petroglyphs that date back to a period known as human prehistory, but constitute a masterful period in the history of the line. What we can say is that their authors were good calligraphers, had 'good handwriting', a desire for style, and control over their drawing, the most remarkable feature of which is the extreme simplicity that contains endless information.

This is what my mother's mouth looks like.

I cannot reproduce fragments of my mother's soliloquies. Needless to say, she only ever talked to herself when she was alone or in the presence of a close relative she assumed was immersed in their own work. María and me, for example, doing our homework. From time to time, the murmur of my mother's stream of consciousness would grow louder, accelerate, even unfold or diverge into different voices that would sometimes argue vociferously with each other. This happened a lot in what might be called 'places of water'. At the kitchen sink or at the place for washing clothes, which might be the local river or the basin my father ended up installing next to the whimsical well. He dug that well for years. He would resume his work every summer, when the well dried up. Until he came across another of those 'false springs' that deceived him and filled him with hope. In this way, he got down to fifteen metres, when his figure would be swallowed up by blackness and he thought he had finally reached the end. Confronted water's Alzheimer's. The story of that well was the story of a failure. He had built a void. He had also built a desire. I always approached that well with shame and resentment. But now I see it as the mouth of literature. I see my father silently digging or dynamiting stones and language in search of his own stream of consciousness.

At the kitchen sink, in the rotating action of hands doing the dishes or the movement of washing in the river, my mother talks to herself in suspense. She murmurs, shares secrets, furiously replies to an impertinence or question. There are times it would have been very interesting to know who she was talking to. There was one particular situation that transformed her whole body. An extreme case of metamorphosis. The rage brought on by injustice. She was never violent, she was well mannered, gentle in speech, of a sunny disposition. But I remember her once in an office of the town hall, tired of being mistreated, swearing she would come back with a rock like the one María Pita threw at the pirate and admiral, Francis Drake. So here is my mother, talking to herself. Her face changes. She grows hot, laughs, her eyes become all atmospheric. They glint, cloud over, flash, remain

The author's mother (on the left) and Aunt Paquita

in misty suspense. All of this has to do with words. There's something going on in the kitchen. I look up from my book or exercises and stare at her, simultaneously amazed and disturbed, not daring to interrupt. If she's opening up like this, it's because she's possibly in a landscape of confidence. I cannot recall what she was saying, probably because at the time I was more concerned with the expressive phenomenon than with the expression itself. My memory is made up of remnants, beads of language that go forwards and back, rotating.

It might be said that at this point my mother was wearing her stream of consciousness on her sleeve. She was an open body. She was talking. And others were talking through her. Who were they? In *Waiting for Godot*, there's a scene in which Vladimir and Estragon hear the low voices of the dead. They make a noise like wings. Like leaves. Like sand. They whisper. They rustle. They murmur.

> VLADIMIR: *To be dead is not enough for them.*
> ESTRAGON: *It is not sufficient.*

No, it is not sufficient. Why does Juan Preciado return to Comala? His mother makes him promise, that's true, in order to reclaim the inheritance of his father, Pedro Páramo. But what is that inheritance in reality? His mother describes the place where she is sending her son like this: 'The air changes the colour of things there. And life whirrs by as quiet as a murmur ... the pure murmuring of life.' Comala may be desolate, but it is not a non-place. On the contrary, it is the place of humanity, as in Kafka's 'Metamorphosis' there is the room of humanity. The place where being dead – or alive! – is not sufficient.

We don't really know what literature is, but we can detect its mouth. Not only in books, but in life as well. This mouth rarely warns us it is going to open. It takes the form of a rumour. A murmur. It can even be closed, covered in earth, wounded, feeling how the words swarm excitedly around it. It can be a mouth that is contorted, painted, voluptuous, dehydrated. It can be scandalous, incontinent, enigmatic, impudent, stuttering. What it doesn't want is to dominate. It is always an eccentric mouth. Alone or in a group, it talks to itself. Its inner movement is that of the dance in which the bodies of words contract or expand while turning. The mouth murmurs Rosalía's poem:

> *Of those footsteps*
> *That they dance now,*
> *Forward and back,*
> *From back to fore.*

Years ago, a friend from Soneira Valley, Roberto Mouzo, an enthusiast of signs in the manuscript of earth, handed me a series of paper reproductions of the petroglyphs on the Death Coast, where there were lots of concentric circles grouped together. These drawings remained on my desk for a long time, turning invisibly around me. One day, I had to fill out one of those questionnaires about the limits of fiction and truth, invention and memory . . . I was both sorry for replying and unhappy with my answers. But the concentric circles were there. Whatever they might mean for experts, for *archaeolatry*, they murmured a response about reality and the way to view it. Reality turned out to be just one of the circles of reality. What a ridiculous piece of reality is seen by those who confuse it with sticky topicality. The optics of enlargement shown by the circles include the inner and outer senses, memory and imagination. In *The Disasters of War*, Goya has a title: 'One Can't Look'. From when we were little, the slogan of fear: 'One Can't Say'. Or: 'That's a sin'.

The mouth said what couldn't be said. It sounded like a sin.

119

The departure point for the expansion of the petroglyph is shaped like the mouth that talks to itself. There it was, fermenting, on tenterhooks, both discovering and creating secrets. The petroglyph of concentric circles took me to an unusual, unpredictable place above time, like the overgrown track to A Cavaxe. To the beginning of the 'Second Manifesto of Surrealism': 'Everything leads to the belief that there exists a certain point of the mind at which life and death, the real and the imaginary, the past and the future, the communicable and the incommunicable, the high and the low, are not perceived as contradictions. It would be vain to attribute to surrealism any other motive than the hope of determining this point.'

The energy source that drives this hope is the insufficient. The simultaneous walking of desire and pain. Like Charlie Chaplin the Tramp, it rests on both of these. The first films we saw were in the Hercules Cinema, in Monte Alto. All of us waiting expectantly in the dark chamber. The whole cinema mimicking the roar of the Metro lion like a liberation. But, before that, we had a logo of our own: the lighthouse casting a beam across the screen that was met with enthusiastic applause. I was very small. From those films, the only images that wash up are those of Tarzan and Charlie Chaplin the Tramp. Down Torre Street, María walked like Chaplin when she was little. This way of walking activates the mouth of imagination and memory. I became acquainted with that mouth very quickly. But I didn't know it had inspired the enigmatic drawing of the concentric circles or been described in the 'Second Manifesto of Surrealism'.

At the time, it was nothing more or less than the mouth of my mother talking to herself.

18

The Glazier and *Long Night*

The first book to enter our house that wasn't a schoolbook was a monumental work. Judging by the title, *Five Thousand Years of History*, by the size and thickness, a real stone slab. One of those works that leave an immortal mark on your head if they land on top of you. My mother bought it in the La Poesía bookshop on Santo André Street. We went down to the city with her and carried that book between us, as if on a platform in procession. Five thousand years of history on the back of humankind. My word, it was heavy! We carried it with a mixture of respect and glee. In particular because of the circumstances in which it was purchased. It was the feast of Our Lady of Mount Carmel, the Virgin of the Sea. We wanted to buy her a gift. Typical presents for mothers were household items. In reality, they weren't for them. They acted as intermediaries. We were thinking of buying her a coffee machine or something like that. And that was when she took us to La Poesía and said, 'Actually, no. This time, we're going to buy a book.'

As a girl, my mother had been a contented, clandestine reader. She knew verses by Rosalía de Castro off by heart, even though her favourite poem, the one that trembled on her lips, was the funeral oration Curros Enríquez dedicated to the author of *New Leaves*, one of the harshest secular psalms in the history of Galicia: 'Ah, of those that wear on their forehead a star! / Ah, of those that wear on their lips a song!' A poem that sums up all this history like the plot of a detective story in which the person who embodied Galicia the best (a contemporary Mother Earth goddess) is devoured by her contemporaries: 'The muse of the peoples / that I saw go by, / she was food for the wolves, / consumed she did die . . . / Of her the bones are / that with you will belong.' We are still living one of the chapters of that nightmare, with the deceased, like Castelao, held under ecclesiastical lock and key in a Pantheon of Illustrious Galicians that isn't even public heritage. Her beyond should be Adina Cemetery, the one she sang about, and Castelao's should be the homeland of exile, La Chacarita, the cemetery with the most bird's nests in the world.

Carme, my mother, had read a lot as a child. Most of all, she'd read the lives of saints. Volumes of exemplary lives that dozed in the darkness of the attic in the vicarage in Corpo Santo. The vicar's niece, Dona Isabel, grew fond of the girl and semi-adopted her. The large Barrós brood had been left without a mother. This Dona Isabel was very special. A suitor had presented her with a parrot, which she baptised Pio Nono and taught Latin. But the Vaticanist parrot, whose cage was on the balcony, soon switched language when it heard the pine-cone collectors from Altamira passing by. It was a fan of the *vox populi* and quickly learned how to swear magnificently. That was until Dona Isabel ordered it to be confined to the attic, where Pio Nono, deprived of speech – a low voice – gazed at the reading girl. My mother, apart from laughing with the parrot, made the most of Dona Isabel's patronage to disappear to the attic, where, alone with books, she would lose all notion of time.

There were no books in our house. But we soon found out

that the house was calling for them. One of the first things my father did when we moved to Castro was subscribe to a newspaper, in this case *La Voz de Galicia*. It was a wonderful period, when the newspaper was directed by Pedro de Llano Bocelo and then by Francisco Pillado. Bocelo was a popular character in a way that few journalists have been in A Coruña. My mother read him with enthusiasm because of his quest for solidarity with the underprivileged. In the hands of my parents, the newspaper really was 'the working man's book'. For my father, it constituted a whole ritual. He would read it very slowly and read it all. The only section he missed out was the section devoted to sport. He hated football so much he wouldn't even shout 'Long live Russia!' when the Spanish national team was playing.

Often, on a Sunday morning, a young man with a book in his hand would climb the hill to O Escorial, in the direction of A Zapateira. We knew his name. This was Chao, Pai-Pai and Felisa's son. He greeted us and carried on towards the unknown. But we children would fix our eyes on what he was carrying in his hand. On the paper creature. The secret.

One morning in winter, on the way to school, Domingos, who was a little older than me, informed me that Chao had been taken prisoner. Prisoner? What for? In a low voice, Domingos then said something that froze my insides: 'One can't say!' How terrible must the crime have been if it couldn't even be expressed in words! What could he have done, this amusing, entertaining young man who took books for walks in the mountains? It was back in 1964. In the newspaper, alongside others, appeared the photo provided by the Political–Social Brigade. Manuel Bermúdez, alias Chao, his face transformed, looking like a bandit. In fact, Chao, who'd been working since he was thirteen, first in a graphite factory and then as a glazier, had been involved in the anti-Fascist struggle since 1959. He was a nonconformist when it came to speech. Including the sentences that served to underline the slamming of cards in the tavern: 'The flies will come and warn you!', 'Go and see if the cat has laid an egg!' or more enigmatic stuff, such as the solemn 'By the beard of Dostoyevsky!' This spirit would explode during carnival, with its popular surrealism: 'The Mass will be on the eighteenth of July if the deceased receive their bonuses. *In saecula saeculorum*, pig meat bacon is!'

One day, in the bar Os Beléns in Monelos, he came across Guillerme, who told him, 'Don't talk so loud! Keep your voice down. There are other things you can do.' Guillerme had just arrived from France. He'd brought some clandestine newspapers, such as *Mundo Obrero*. Off they went, on the Guzzi, to deliver it around districts and villages in the shadows. For years, those young men on their motorbike managed to escape the eye that saw everything. Chao lived the experience with fear and emotion.

Carnival in Castro de Elviña

There was a lot of indifference and distrust. But in the most unexpected, isolated places, there would be a hand in the night impatiently awaiting the secret pages.

In A Coruña Prison, a group of political prisoners organised a kind of free school, open to ordinary inmates. One day, Chao read a newspaper cutting that said, 'The dangerous offender against private property Suso the Scorpion has been arrested.' The following day, the Scorpion entered prison. Those who knew him welcomed the recidivist: 'The Scorpion's back, the Scorpion's back!' He enrolled in the makeshift school. He was really quite innocent by nature. Chao asked him, 'What are you here for, Suso?' And he explained, 'This time, for stealing manure.' Chao found the metaphor difficult to believe: the dangerous offender was in prison for having stolen a cart of manure. The Scorpion added, 'But I didn't tell the police I had stashed away some treasure.' The Scorpion was a likeable character. The theft of manure didn't go to court, however, and the order came to set him free. They threw him out, so to speak. The treasure man cried when taking his leave of the clandestine school, 'I have such a good time here. You have tobacco and everything!' In prison, Chao also came into contact with some tricksters who had swindled Hispano Americano Bank out of a fortune. They were Argentinian, elegant in appearance; they looked like dandies. Their food in prison was brought to them from an expensive restaurant that served platefuls of seafood. They would discuss the injustices of the economic system. While tucking into goose barnacles, the virtuoso swindlers would rebuff Chao – who was trying to explain the alliance between the forces of work and culture – by saying, 'You really are a bunch of idiots! Where's the money? In the banks! Go after it!! That's the way to fight capitalism!'

*   *   *

When he came out of prison, we saw Chao again on a Sunday, on his way to the mountains, with a book in his hand. It didn't take María and me long to set out after him. The title of the book was *Long Night of Stone* by Celso Emilio Ferreiro. That day, thanks to the youthful glazier, we were able to see wounded words emerging from under the stones. When a state of emergency was declared or there was a strike or the regime was sharpening its claws, Chao would disappear. He'd already said he wasn't going to lounge around in bed, waiting to be arrested again. María and I used to visit a cave, an old mud pit. We'd go with a bucket to fetch clay so María could make some figures. If you didn't know it was there, it was difficult to find. The entrance to the cave was narrow and obscured by bracken. It was nice being inside. Seeing the mouth of light, feeling its glow inside the earth. A warm, damp chamber with the welcoming, ancestral smell of mud. One day, we came across a checkered blanket folded up in a corner. On top of it was a book, one of those books that still talk, half read: *The Brothers Karamazov*. So this was the room of humanity, the cave we could perhaps return to one day as a refuge.

We never told anyone about it. Not even our mother, who would have sent us back with milk and bread for the mysterious tramp. Not even Chao. By the beard of Dostoyevsky!

126

19

Heraclitus, Parmenides and the Co-ed Institute

We were standing up on the worn velvet seats of the old Monelos Cinema. Dancing wildly to 'Los chicos con las chicas'. Los Bravos made a film from that song that was such a hit at the end of the 1960s. But we had a special reason for shouting out the elementary refrain: 'Boys and girls have to be together!' The institute in Monelos was the first co-ed institution in the whole of Galicia. It was located in a border area, where new blocks of social housing met fields of maize. A revolution. A frenzy. Sometimes, groups of pupils from private, religious schools would come to witness the spectacle. Boys and girls leaving class together. Bell-bottoms, the first miniskirts. But, above all, the excitement of being together. Suddenly establishing a connection with a look while the teacher Caeiro explains an essential debate that permeates the whole of history. Either you're Parmenides. Everything remains. Or you're Heraclitus. Everything flows: you never bathe in the same river twice.

Heraclitus was right, said Caeiro, but Parmenides wasn't wrong.

The river, girl. Bathe together, girl. Remain, flow. It's all in the classics.

I ran. I always had a strong wish to attend that school. In my feet and in my head. I would go across country as far as Elviña. Cross the Avenue like a Viet Cong. Officially named Alfonso Molina, back then it was called 'the Ho Chi Minh route'. Lots of people got run over there until they finally built a footbridge. One of those who died was Manuel of Corpo Santo, my grandfather the scribe. This keen walker wasn't killed in the war, but ended up being knocked over by a car on the Avenue. A poacher. The driver made off. And Manuel was stranded in the ditch, at the hour that separates the dog from the wolf. I ran in order to cross that mined frontier every day. I then followed a path that bordered the railway, next to a sea of rye. Until I reached the 'district of flowers', an area with blocks of social housing that were worthy of the name. There was an architectonic imagination that had envisaged something different and lacked the prison-like appearance of other new estates. This co-ed institute wasn't just an exotic destination for peeping Toms. It was also a centre of attraction for juvenile gangs, the most famous being the Red Devils. They would go there more in search of fun than action. They would sometimes turn up with a portable record player, and the playground would transform into a party. In a way, they belonged to the institute. They should have been pupils, but they weren't, even though there were some who were both 'within and without'. I was struck by the hierarchy that existed in these groups. Their leadership wasn't just a question of strength. One of the bosses was the Chinaman, who was short and light as a fly, but had the most intimidating eyes. So you had to try not to look at him, because, if you did, you soon felt the blade of his tongue scraping the back of your neck: 'Hey, you, what you looking at?' With the support of the group, he dominated by means of his cruelty. He carried a set of screwdrivers in the

128

pocket of his sheepskin jacket. There was another kind of leader whose charisma came from the enchantment aroused by dangerous beauty. This was the case with Miguel the Palavean. His appearance always took the form of a ghostly apparition. Thin, olive skin, jet-black hair, full of laughter, aware of his charm, he provoked immediate uproar, in which there was a mixture of expectation and caution. It was him, really, it was him! But it seems true that the gods punish the chosen. Life would be hard on those who were hard. A mirror full of scars.

I ran towards that place. I would have gone on Sundays if it had been open. I spent seven years at the co-ed institute: the six years of my baccalaureate and the one year of university orientation. It was on the side of the mountain, surrounded by meadows and fields, behind Oza Church. The first few years, it was little more than a shed with a flimsy roof and walls, always looking like a temporary shelter that fought bravely against the storms. What ever happened to Heraclitus, Parmenides, and the girl who bathed in the river?

With María and others by the Tower of Hercules

For us, studying was a rash adventure. I mean for María and me. We were pushed by our primary school teachers, Don Antonio and Dona Fina. But this divided the family. It was uncommon back then for the children of a working-class family to continue their studies after school. My father wasn't sure about this. And now I understand him. He saw me working on a building site and had already found a job for María as a sales assistant in a shoe shop. Not bad, right? She went to try it out for two weeks. One day, she came back from work and said, 'I'm not going anymore. I want to be a student.' María, when she was clear about something, wouldn't budge. She had the soul of a suffragette. So students we were. She enrolled in A Milagrosa, a public institution that had links with the provincial orphanage. In the fourth year of her baccalaureate, María won a writing competition sponsored by a soft drinks manufacturer, in which all the teaching centres took part. First in A Coruña. Then in the whole of Spain. Her prize was a trip to Puerto Rico. The headline in the newspapers: 'Bricklayer's Daughter Wins National Writing Competition.' That story by María, written when she was fourteen, was an unusual text imbued with beautiful harshness. The life of a tree, its felling, its journey to be cut into pieces in a sawmill. The kind of story that makes you ask, 'How is this possible?' A year after the award, María got rid of the presents she'd been given. Everything except for a few records of Puerto Rican music and a book of Tagore's collected poems. She burned everything in the garden, under my mother's silent gaze. My mother knew that freedom could hurt. A free woman was growing inside María, whose eyes were getting bigger and bigger, like bell jars. She didn't stop crying the day of the coup in Chile, with the death of Salvador Allende. There were those who knew the reason, and others who asked, 'But what's wrong with the child?' My mother kept quiet.

We had friends in common, who would pass each other on the way. Lots of them studied in Monelos. The place of studies coincided with the place of desire. The erotic place. The contrast between 'place' and 'non-place' is often a topic of discussion. There is 'the other place', where a second life is born. Something happened there. A psychogeographical concordance, a special set of teachers and a generation of stammering rebelliousness that wanted to say what one couldn't say.

At the co-ed institute, we requested the hall for a free activity organised by pupils. The most daring group in the Monelos crew – Celsa, Xoana, Chuqui and Luciano – recited a poem by Bertolt Brecht that could well have been the slogan of those times: 'How the Ship *Oskawa* Was Taken Apart by Her Crew'. We played records by Voces Ceibes. And interpreted *The Peasant's Catechism* by Valentín Lamas Carvajal, that prodigy of insurgent humour written by a blind man at the end of the nineteenth century:

– *Are you a peasant?*
– *Yes, for my sins.*

The one asking the questions, the one playing the priest, was Pedro Morlán. And I was the peasant. Morlán made a very good confessor. Perhaps because of his presence – that of a tall, pale, thin, revolutionary young man. The ideal, the revolutionary dream, was in the air. There were some conservative teachers, but they were generally the most eccentric. Even the priests were Reds. First of all, Don Maurilio. And Rodríguez Pampín, who came later, timid in appearance, always deep in thought, the stony weight of the sky on his head. The complete opposite of Don Maurilio, who was a small, fibrous, electric kind of man. It seemed the whole of his body was at the service of his voice. For upholding masterly lessons or sermons with the salt of the earth. Through this priest, the son of peasant farmers in Castile, we learned about Hélder Câmara, the archbishop of Olinda and Recife who opened the way for liberation theology, about Ernesto Cardenal, and Camilo Torres, the Colombian guerrilla priest; we also learned the basic concepts of structuralism and psychoanalysis. The roots of a community were established. We saw through to the other side of scripture. Had Christ returned, he would have been crucified again on the spot. All you had to do was see the processions during Holy Week. But watching Don Maurilio demonstrate the existence of God by means of the atheist philosopher Althusser, who was very fashionable back then in intellectual circles, was no lesser spectacle. I say 'watch' because he used the blackboard a lot for his diagrams of Marxist structuralism, but always kept them within the limits of the blackboard. God appeared above the blackboard, on the throne of his superstructure. The most convincing argument that dispelled any doubts about faith was watching him play pelota. This stocky priest would roll up his sleeves and be transformed into pure, invincible infrastructure. With the co-ed institute surrounded by the jeeps of the Armed Police, the so-called 'greys', these priests had the courage to say a funeral mass for two shipyard workers shot dead at a demonstration in Ferrol on 10 March 1972. Pampín spoke Galician. And spoke inwardly. If Maurilio's God was a historical optimist at the forefront of constructivism, for whom Bauhaus could be a continuation of Genesis, one imagined Pampín's God as a vulnerable, existentialist being who was willing to shake hands with uneasy Nothingness, a creator more in need of protection than almighty. I went to the boarding house where he lived, a very modest room in Catro Camiños. He handed me a book and said, 'Keep it hidden under your jersey and don't take it out until you get home.' It was *Forever in Galicia* by Alfonso Castelao, published in exile in America and known as the Galician Bible. A book that was used to being hidden and saying the things one couldn't say. With humour and pain. Written by a man who was losing his sight. Aged, defeated, smothered by the advance of Nazism, suffering from survivor's guilt, Castelao watches from his room, at dusk, how the windows of the buildings in Manhattan light up. He is exhausted. Alone. He writes, 'I am the child of an unknown country.' But something extraordinary happens. A groundswell. Chaplin's walk. He goes to Harlem. It's winter. He sketches a young black tramp. Possibly the best portrait of his life. 'Listen,' says my mother with the secular Bible in her hand, 'what is Galicia's Holy Trinity? The cow, the fish, the tree.' Both priests, Maurilio and Pampín, were kind at a time that wasn't. The Church wasn't kind to them, felled as they were like trees.

Something else happened back then. Franco's secret police, the Political–Social Brigade, paid a visit to the management of the co-ed institute. The acts of the ship *Oskawa* being taken apart by her crew on a Saturday came to an end, as did our experience of the freedom of the press on a cyclostyle. The management said it was for our own good. They were nice people. Teaching us a lesson. An intense, historical immersion. Now, it was fear's turn. But we had already tasted freedom, the greatest sin in Spain. What one cannot say had infiltrated our molars. We had heard Michael Servetus on the lips of our teacher Caeiro: '*Libertatem meam mecum porto.*' I carry my freedom with me. At the exit of the co-ed institute, there was always an ashen car containing men with an oblique glance. The Suburban Free Institute, the boys and girls, were under scrutiny.

20

A Job Where You Don't Get Wet

'Son, can't you find yourself a job where you don't get wet!'

Apart from attending the co-ed institute, I tried to prepare myself as well as I could to carry out my mother's mandate. Among other things, I went to a typing school. There is a poem by Pedro Salinas in which he calls the keys 'happy girls'. I felt that happiness the first day I sat down in front of the keyboard. My fingers were sluggish, they got the levers all mixed up, but everything changed when the typing tutor came up, positioned my fingers on the keys and pressed down to give them the necessary impetus, the gentle motive force that would propel the carriage and the walk of universal writing. To do this, she stood behind you, embraced your shoulders and took control of your hands to turn the fingers into well-informed, walking operatives. Hers was a corporal kind of speech in which words, fragrant skin and locks formed part of a unique language whose accent was on your fingertips. I never thought typing could be so erotic. My fingers picked up speed: light, happy and Bohemian. I was sorry not to progress to shorthand, but I had to find myself a job where I wouldn't get wet.

The day I climbed the stairs to the offices of the *Ideal Gallego*,

I didn't know whether I wanted to be a journalist, only that I wanted to be a writer. At the time, I wrote verses, which I thought were poems, in among my maths numbers and equations. When the teacher came over, I would conceal the secret with my hands and body. The poem curled up like a hedgehog. But one day he discovered it, the poem, the open hedgehog. His reaction was to read it, his thick lenses surveying that strange creature, the surprised hedgehog, a poem among numbers. I was expecting a telling-off, not a verdict. But what he said was, 'Why do they always write sad things?' I cannot remember how sad it was, the poem, that hedgehog advancing with its own unanswered questions between rows of equations, but I do remember being taken aback by the way he used the plural to identify me. I wrote poems. I wrote sad poems. I belonged to a strange tribe that wrote sad poems. Perhaps the problem was in the nuance. I didn't get around to explaining to him that the poem was sad, but the way I'd written it was happy. The hedgehog was learning how to type.

In the psychogeography of those times, there are other unforgettable places where the hedgehog uncurled. One was the library in San Carlos Gardens, in the Old City. It was a long way from Monelos, after class. I used to go there via the port, which I entered from A Palloza. The port was an open area back then. One could enjoy the most beautiful architecture: ships and cranes. The work of netters spinning and mending their large marine cobwebs. The boisterous voices of those returning alive from their combat in the Gran Sol. On the stage set of the sky, above the bay, the most exhilarating spectacle was the clouds of starlings sketching cartoons to confuse the birds of prey. Some of those clouds of starlings would alight in the circular San Carlos Gardens. As would the more or less sad poets among us. Not far from there, they opened the first pub in A Coruña: Dylan's. Thanks to Carlos, the brave man who came up with the idea, this was a small establishment that dreamed towards the future like vinyl. A place of discovery. You could immerse yourself every day in the wilderness of music and people saying all the things one couldn't say. It also belonged to the geography of the other place, where you heard things you'd never heard before. Even the unexpected. All that complicit music, the unending, runaway kiss with that mysterious girl, a bit cross-eyed and hoarse, merged with the startling power of María Callas in 'La mamma morta'.

Sorridi e spera! Io son l'amore!

Dylan's was the room of humanity. A nomadic home. Forward and back, from back to fore. A small place in the Old City, fighting bravely. Against fines. The sanctions that forced them to close for a while. Some afternoons, you would arrive and the door would be locked. Not a whisper. On the corner, the crooked silhouette of a secret policeman. Where had the songs gone? The dry leaves in San Carlos Gardens, drawing circles on the vinyl of the ground, in the wake of the cross-eyed girl.

'Are you going?'

'I have work to do. I mustn't be late.'

'Don't go!'

I left. With my head down. The stigma of the accursed race. Work. I never saw her again.

Vivi ancora! Io son la vita!

I wanted to be a writer, but what kind of profession was that? Most of the writers I admired had earned a living on a newspaper. From Mark Twain to Graciliano Ramos, the Brazilian who wrote *Barren Lives*. Hey! Try not to quote so much. Don't overdo the quotes. Learn to quote without inverted commas. Remember the time you attended a conference by a Famous Writer. He read his speech with a certain lack of enthusiasm. Someone from the public asked him which authors had influenced him most. He began to pluck names out of the air, with growing excitement: Shakespeare, Cervantes, the great English novel, the great Russian novel, the great French novel, Faulkner of course, not forgetting Valle-Inclán . . . The ironic mouth of literature sounds from the audience, 'What fault is it of theirs that you write?' In A Coruña, there was a strong tradition of throwing barbs. And people with a good aim, who were courageous. A recital by the leader of the Falangist poetry group Amanecer (Dawn) was interrupted at the crucial moment by a shout of 'Another plate of squid!'

At the co-ed institute, we edited a magazine that ended up being clandestine. I interviewed heterodox mouths of local culture. One that led to another. The playwright Manuel Lourenzo, imprisoned in his youth; the musician Miro Casabella, grandson of a blind singer of ballads; the humorist and comics writer Chichi Campos, whose every panel was subversive . . . Many couldn't be published, but they formed part of the freedom I carried with me. A casual coincidence, the hasty exit from a concert by Miro that hadn't been approved by the governor, allowed me to meet Toño López Mariño. It was like meeting Bugs Bunny and Jack Kerouac at the same time. Toño had gone from the lesser seminary of Santiago to the Beat Generation in a single jump. He was one of the last to graduate from the school of journalism in Madrid and signed his chronicles with the initials WBS (Why Bother Signing). I told him my story, and he suggested I drop by the *Ideal Gallego*. This ancient journal of Catholic intransigence was going through a period of intense change, with a new director, Rafael González, from Andalusia. It wasn't quite on a level with *Combat*. There was an old, very conservative guard on the staff, but there were others who subscribed to and practised principles and obligations of journalism like those espoused by Albert Camus. Not to lie. To confess what you do not know. To stand up against any kind of despotism, whatever the excuse . . . In short, not to dominate. Xosé Antón Gaciño, Luís Pita and Gabriel Plaza were new reference points in the world of Galician journalism. They were the ones who would occasionally be insulted on the stairs to the *Ideal* by extremists who called themselves the Warriors of Christ the King. The *Ideal*'s new soul was altering the way information was presented, much to the chagrin of the Fascist authorities and reactionary clergy, who observed with increasing amazement how their old parish newsletter was sprouting wings. But that wasn't all. The journalists contributed to the city's cultural awakening. They organised the first serious retrospective of work by Urbano Lugrís, the seascape surrealist. When you see one of his pictures, you think the sea exists in part so that Lugrís could paint it. He used to say he painted in underwater workshops like a solitary companion of Captain Nemo. It was the summer of 1975. We were carrying the pictures one by one under our arms to the Association of Artists. He endured the drama of having to paint the inside of the *Azor*, Franco's yacht, with sea motifs. He then got drunk. They say his best works were done in red wine on the marble tables of different taverns. I remember now. We're walking in a line, each of us embracing a Lugrís, when we come across the extremists roaming free in María Pita Square. Armed with chains. They have no way of knowing what pictures we're carrying under our arms, but we realise that to them they represent potential rubbish, degenerate art, simply because we're the ones carrying them. Gabriel Plaza mutters, 'Don't look at them, keep going.' I'm not a street brawler, I know this, but I feel a strange force emanating from the picture. I could protect it with my body to the end.

But that hasn't happened yet. I am climbing the stairs to the *Ideal*. Not the main ones, but the ones at the back that led straight to the editorial office. There was no control post or private security. In those years of upheaval, editorial offices were marketplaces. The door opened, and in would come a neighbourhood committee, a trade union representative, a group of women shellfish-gatherers wanting to know whether there were any men with the balls to publish their complaints. There were people with news on top of their heads. Live news, news in kind. Now I'm the one climbing the stairs. Nobody sees me. To gain confidence, I climb two steps and go down one, climb two, go down one. I have the staircase syndrome even before I've gone up it. Why did I leave my poems in the office? They're not good, and they're sad as well. I should go back for my poems. Please excuse me, I made a mistake. I have other texts, journalistic texts. I have also carried out a few interviews for the school magazine. What's that about the poems? Please let me explain. My godfather has a typewriter. It's a portable typewriter, very small. He's a travelling salesman, a seller of spices. By the way, did you know that a kilo of saffron is worth more than a kilo of gold? He uses the machine to write his invoices, so the carriage is very short. He wants me to be a cultured man, to be useful. He told me years ago, 'Write if you want, write using the typewriter.' So I started to write, of course I did, like someone playing with letters. What do I write? The carriage is short. I think. Let me write some verses. Lines that look like verses. Poetry. This is how my poetic vocation began. It was determined by the size of the carriage. A game. Children's stuff. You'd better give me back the poems. It might lead to preju-dice, confusion and so on. I don't want to publish poems. I want a job where I don't get wet.

I have some sad poems and my notebook from the co-ed institute. The one who opens the door and does not close it, but welcomes me in, glancing inquisitively at the sheaf of poems, is a young woman by the name of Ánxela Souto, the director's secretary. I don't know about magic, but magical causality certainly exists. My first poems find a home in her hands. I feel like Charlie Chaplin after a groundswell. In the best place possible. I come back a week later. Just a moment, please. The director will see you. The director? Yes, that's him, the director. 'Somebody read your poems,' he informs me. 'Said they weren't bad.' This could make for a good title: 'Poems That Are Not Bad'. The most generous review I've ever received. But nothing can beat what he says after that: 'Stick around for a couple of days! Let's see what you can do!'

I left school and, without telling anybody, went running to my first job. I climbed the stairs two by two, opened the door to the editorial office. In the circles of keys, the 'happy girls' were dancing, propelling iron machines. There was the factory of words. The large office where rumours took shape. The rhythm of traction, the writing's advance on the carriage, produced columns of smoke. There were slow ones, thick and dark, that didn't quite take off, forming a cloud of nostalgia around their author. Others that rose with artistic calm, forming arabesques before throwing themselves at the blades of the fans. And then fleet-footed ones, the swift, direct smoke of furious writing.

Almost all the journalists smoked. The typewriters had small metal ashtrays soldered on to the side. It was fine to know how to type, but if you wanted to be a real journalist, the first thing you had to do was buy some tobacco. In among the clouds, along the central aisle, Ánxela led me to a desk. She sat me down in front of a man with oversleeves of the kind worn by old journalists. He was a frail, silent man, so I wasn't surprised when he handed me a typewritten sheet and said with a conjuror's solemn irony, 'Make it intelligible and give it a headline of fewer than ten words.' On looking closely at the sheet, a correspondent's chronicle, I realised it was a copy of the carbon copy. It was hard to make out the words, which carbon shadows only hinted at. A couple of days. Something to do. More than I could dream of. There's no pay. I'm an apprentice. It's the first time I've heard this word. It sounds ancient. I hear people saying, 'Get the apprentice to do it.' The apprentice, I wonder to myself. Who can that be? Until I realise the arrow is aimed at me. I am the apprentice. I still don't know whether it sounds good or bad.

The veteran's name was Javier Guimaraens. A legend on the old *Ideal*, responsible for local information about towns and municipalities. Very austere in everything, including in the way he expressed himself. His extreme thinness may have had something to do with the obsessive practice of pruning texts. He was a very conservative man. Even to identify himself, he didn't need long sentences. On that first day, he looked at me over his glasses, like an entomologist sizing up an unknown specimen on the other side of the desk. We never collided after that. He was highly respectful and taught me a lot about verbal paucity. I followed my instinct, focusing on headlines of fewer than ten words and on my job as a palaeologist poring over municipal texts.

One of the apprentice's first missions was to be the bearer of news. I mean this literally. A lot of chronicles from local correspondents arrived by coach. There was no bus station, so you had to go to the different stops and the drivers would hand you an envelope. Chronicles by phone, reversing the charges, were only acceptable in extreme cases, such as a serious accident.

I handed the municipal envelopes to Guimaraens and sat down to wait for new challenges in the world of journalistic conjuring. There were texts that were written by hand, in scrawly, complicated handwriting. Others that possessed an admirable desire for style, laborious, calligraphic poems whose spirit flagged

141

in order to inform us of the coming visit of the Provincial Delegate for Choirs and Dances of Education and Rest of the National Movement's Women's Section. In these cases, it was necessary to type them out. Those that were already typed had to be revised, corrected and sometimes abridged so they would fit the space available. Needless to say, they had to be given a headline of fewer than ten words. Some chroniclers made their feelings known. For them, aside from bold type, a successful headline was a long one that told the whole story. I turned into a fan of Guimaraens's minimalism and gobbled up more and more words.

One day, my immediate, minimalist boss handed me a sheet. He didn't even look at me or open his mouth. By the format and other marks, I quickly identified its source. It was a chronicle from Boiro by a correspondent who signed himself 'Enmuce'. Enmuce was highly reliable. And very hard-working. He used to send in a chronicle almost every day. The problem was that he sent the same chronicle to every newspaper. Most correspondents were not paid. Their only compensation was being published. In contemporary language, we might say it formed a 'virtual payment'. Enmuce used carbon paper to make copies. But there were lots of copies. Up to seven. Things got really complicated when you received one of the last copies. But this had never happened before. Not until today. Not being able to understand a single word. It was the end of summer. My reputation really was on the line now. Including the job in which I didn't get wet.

I had to use the opposite technique to minimalism. What it says, more or less, in the Icelandic *Edda*: 'The first word will lead to the second, and the second to the third.' The chronicle was in Spanish, and the first word identified itself, even gestured to be seen: '*patata*'. Little by little, using the carbon signs that were visible and the traces of the keys, I managed to decipher the unknown territory. To weave the words together. Certain words led to others. I felt that the words that had disappeared wanted to return to life. They were peering out from behind the keys. I reassembled this chronicle that spoke of the discovery of a gigantic potato on the very day a UFO had been spotted in the area. Unidentified Flying Objects were very fashionable back then. There'd even been a government directive ordering the restriction of news about UFOs, since they might unsettle the local population and question the heavenly order. But the news about a UFO and a gigantic tuber, now that was hot stuff.

The correspondent was congratulated. And I carried on waiting for further messages from the outer system.

21

A Normal Person

The deadline. The deadline was sacred. If we were late closing, we would miss the connections. The connections were the crucial points in the newspaper's distribution. A dense network of strategic crossroads on the map of Galicia. In cities, it was easy to make up for a delay. But the war was being waged in towns and villages, in a territory with the most widely dispersed population in Europe. It was here, at the connection points, where our own vans passed the baton to coaches and all kinds of vehicles – some private – that completed the route. You had to be there at the agreed time. Being late was not an excuse. Mist, rain, snow, gales, formed part of normality. It wasn't a convincing argument for a driver to attribute missing a connection to the Great Flood. There was always a way through.

'A connection has been missed in Ortigueira!'

Missing a connection was a real drama in the life of a newspaper. A defeat. A mournful statistic. Because there was a struggle back then, copy by copy, to defend or even take small positions. Large maps of Galicia hung on the walls, some of them in relief, inhabited by a dense mass of coloured pins. In red, the points where the real battle was taking place: the critical connections.

One night, in the editorial office, things got complicated. By the time I realised, there was no one to give me a lift. I had no money for a taxi. The weather was bad. The house in Castro was a long way to go walking through the storm. It was a shame I hadn't gone with Toño. One Friday, leaving the office, he had invited me along. His parents had a bar, Dos Ciudades, on the border between the Old City and the Fish Market. They lived on a floor of the same building. A small floor occupied by beds. Toño had five sisters. And there were the five girls, laughing amongst themselves, laughing at me. 'But he's just a baby! He looks as if he's just come out of a seminary!' How nice, what a lovely surprise, how dizzy it made me feel, to hear so much laughter and to be laughed at. I swore I would return. But not on this occasion.

So I hid in the office. Slept in a phone booth, lying on paper, covered in a jacket. The telephone was up above me, high, mute, taciturn, alert. What would I do if it rang? What if it was the news of the year and I was the only one there, in the right place, at the right time? I still hadn't worked out whether I would answer or not when I fell asleep. On top of the papers. I was a real journalist now. I was woken in the morning by the singing of the cleaning lady. Without being seen, I went to the toilet and then sat down at a desk, pretending to have something urgent to do. Everything was fine until the deputy director, Juan Molina, turned up and was met by the head of administration. I should say the 'all-powerful boss', as teletypes referred to the union leader Jimmy Hoffa. He was furious. Something terrible had happened. I listened in. My heart thumping away. What terrible thing could have happened? I wasn't the culprit, but, whatever it was, I could be a suspect.

'We missed a connection in Pontedeume!' said the thundering voice.

'We closed on time,' replied Molina in a low voice.

'Well, close before time!'

I breathed a sigh of relief. But that day I thought someone should write an underground history of journalism. That talked about exile and censorship, yes. But with a chapter devoted to connections and the men and women in delivery. There was so much pressure I would sometimes envisage writing an article that paid tribute to the heroes of distribution. 'In the history of western media, there is nothing like the extraordinary network set up for the distribution of newspapers in Galicia. Not even the legendary Pony Express reached such a level of precision and efficiency in its connections.'

In life, you should never miss your connections.

There's another lesson my university teachers never taught me, and I never heard at conferences or read in books by media experts. The importance of obituaries for printed newspapers. In particular, the paid kind: funeral notices. As far as I'm aware, nobody has ever published a funeral notice on the Internet. At the *Ideal*, as at every newspaper, the editorial deadline was sacred. The pressure from the all-powerful administration was very strong, owing to the dramatic war waged over connections. But at night, at the critical moment, it was the manager of the printing press who had the last word. During the day, a serious, polite man, something that is generally said about those who maintain an intimidating silence. The manager's humour and features would gradually change as the deadline approached, foreshadowing the moment when this silent man would turn into a ruthless foreman.

If memory lets go and descends the stairs from the editorial office to the printing room, it will no longer be able to deal with anything other than the fresh aroma coming from cast words. The letters – what was written upstairs, truths and lies galloping over the keys – are now leaden. This is one of my madeleines.

The way the words smelled of lead. Or, to be more precise, the way they smelled of lead and milk. Because there were the lino-typists, sitting in front of the large machines, sculpting out language, each with a bottle of milk at their side. Because words, even true ones, intoxicate bodies. Whenever I could, I would go down there, sometimes to collect the first copies from the rotary machine, when the ink would smudge and tattoo headlines onto your hands. I would go down there because, for me, the real smell of a newspaper, apart from the smoke of typewriter tobacco, was a mixture of lead, milk and ink down in the printing room.

Yes, a time came when all authority was vested in the manager of the printing press, and there was only one thing that could stop the frenetic process that led to the rotary machine starting up: a funeral notice. For as long as possible, someone would remain on call in administration to hire out these funereal spaces that were charged by module, by surface area, at a higher rate than commercial publicity. With a procedure that was non-nego-tiable. You had to pay up front. This was the first time I heard the expression 'pay in cash'.

'Funeral notices are paid for in cash!'

This may have served to underline their essential nature. There was no arguing over stuff that was paid for in cash. Nobody ever discussed the contents of a funeral notice. Or the price. The paper could wait for a while if somebody called the hotline to say they were on their way because of an unexpected death.

At the time, there was some speculation over the demise of local and regional newspapers. The difficulties such papers would have to survive. Taking part in a European survey, the writer Álvaro Cunqueiro, who was director of the *Faro de Vigo*, was the only one, together with the director of *Sud-Ouest*, to question this catastrophic vision: 'I don't know what will happen to other newspapers, but the *Faro de Vigo* – with classified ads in the bows and funeral notices in the stern – is a ship that will never sink.' And the truth is they are still sailing. *Sud-Ouest* with its equivalent: the *avis d'obsèques*. Death in Galicia, when it comes down to it, is still advertised on paper and paid for in cash. The deceased don't trust virtual reality.

I hadn't realised the importance of death notices or those unwritten rules in the functioning of a newspaper until the case of my interview with Luís Seoane. My own, very private case. The first time I experienced with real anxiety the existence or non-existence of a text. Seoane was not just a great artist. He had been an essential reference point during the Galician exile and continued to play that role in the intellectual resistance to Franco. He had a house in Buenos Aires, but had started travelling to Galicia and Spain more frequently after setting up a new ceramics factory in Sargadelos, together with Isaac Díaz Pardo. This duo also had plans to found a newspaper, *Galicia*, that would recover and renew enlightened, democratic, autonomist ideals crushed by Franco's regime. So Luís Seoane was in A Coruña, inaugurating an exhibition at a new gallery. I had just started as an apprentice at the *Ideal*, a publication with a history that ruffled feathers in newspaper libraries, the official spokesperson for the most intransigent brand of National Catholicism. But things were changing quickly. An internal revolution had enraged the board of directors, the National Association of Catholic Propagandists. I proposed an interview with Luís Seoane. Finally, as dusk fell, Gabriel Plaza, editor-in-chief, gave me the green light. Seoane himself was taken aback by this appearance. He knew nothing about me, obviously. But he knew a lot about the *Ideal*, a paper that was widely associated with ignorance or war. He agreed to talk, but was on the defensive to begin with. This may have made the interview more difficult for me, but also more interesting. Thinking about Keats's poem, I asked him about the place today of truth and beauty, and he replied in a flash, 'Beauty can also be terrible.' It was drizzling when I left, and the flagstones in Cantóns glowed with the reflection of banking neon. I ran all the way to the editorial office. It was almost empty. I wrote without looking at my notes, obeying the unconfessable maxim of journalism that says, 'If you forget, invent. And you'll be right!' If you invent well, that is. The manager of the printing press appeared upstairs, following the trail of that somnambulant typing. I was almost unknown to him. Before he could speak, I shouted out with anxious fervour:

'It's an interview with Luís Seoane!'

He chewed over some words. Then said in a loud voice:

'I don't suppose it's for today?'

'Yes, yes. Here it is!' I proclaimed triumphantly.

I wrote out the headline by hand. He took the text. And, as he left, said:

'It may not go in. We're waiting on a funeral notice.'

I waited. I'd learned to smoke by then. I already had the property of a cloud. Every time a door squeaked, I expected it to be the relations with a sackload of money urgently collected in the early hours of the morning. Every last peseta had to be counted. But they didn't come. And eventually the manager of the printing press gave the go-ahead. I was already downstairs. He looked at me. 'That interview's in.' He didn't look unhappy. I think he liked the fact that someone from editorial had gone downstairs to get his hands dirty.

*   *   *

The summer was the best time for an apprentice. There was a veteran journalist, Ezequiel Pérez Montes, who beat all the records. He was capable of interviewing eight of Franco's ministers in a single day, which left the special envoys feeling amazed. He kept his distance. He was a celebrity in the city! But for me it was a real spectacle watching him in action. I remember the day he interviewed a local painter, who was always fishing around for compliments. And Ezequiel asked him:

'Where would you like to be hung, master?'

All that was missing was the noose. The man replied straight from his heart:

'In the Louvre, of course.'

Most editors went on holiday in the summer. So the apprentice ended up doing a bit of everything. Port information. The sensation you were really constructing a poem, with the names of ships docking or leaving. Accident and crime reports. That detective formula I always thought would make a great start to a novel: 'Proceedings have been instituted in the case.' To institute proceedings – what else is literature, if not this?

Some days, I wrote the horoscope, but that was far from easy. Whenever I saw somebody else doing it, whenever I read it, I thought it was a joke. So off I went. But I knew people who were Libra or Pisces or . . . In fact, I knew people who were every sign, including my own. What if I harmed somebody or infused a wretch with false hope? There is a Galician proverb: 'Nobody ever saw the day after today.' I realised you are compromised by the things you write. A horoscope is committed literature as well.

* * *

During that apprenticeship, there was upheaval in the political institutions. Democratic or anti-Fascist organisations were hunted down. Sometimes, at night, you would hear a whisper at the door. The journalists from Political Information went out. They encountered people in a hurry, with a clandestine communiqué and the wake of being prison fodder. One of those who came to the staircase was Moncho Reboiras, who was later shot down by Franco's police in Ferrol. There was a writer named Margarita Ledo working on the *Ideal* at the time. She suddenly disappeared. Portugal had just gone through the Carnation Revolution of 25 April 1974. One day, I was asked, 'Could you take a bag of personal effects for someone who has to flee?' I was given the address and went. Margarita was the one leaving. She was going to steal across the border on her way to exile in Portugal. We embraced. A little later, the government police arrested Gaciño. His chronicle of political life on a Sunday was the most widely read in Galicia by people on both sides of the fence. The Catholic paper's analyst was accused by the governor of being no more and no less than the brains of the democratic opposition in Galicia. What Gaciño *was* was a good journalist. He carried everything around in his head, that much was true. The regime, despite its panoptic eye, was taking more and more stabs in the dark. The demise of the dictatorship was in sight, but it was that dangerous moment when fear engenders fear. In the evening, a group of journalists went to demonstrate in front of the civil governor's residence and delivered a statement in which we denounced the witch-hunt and asked for the prisoner to be released. There must have been a dozen democratic journalists protesting in front of the gate, but we felt like more, especially when Luís Pita opened his mouth and out came the voice of Max Estrella in *Bohemian Lights*: 'Bastards. And they are the ones who protest against the Black Legend of Spain!'

There are times when a few people seem like more. As in a shipwreck.

I don't feel nostalgia for that time. 'Nostalgia is what dogs have if you take away their bone,' said the freethinker António Sérgio in order to have a go at the chief apostle of *saudosismo*, the poet Teixeira de Pascoaes. What I do feel is a certain nostalgia for being an apprentice. Because the apprentice could come and go without being seen. He was an invisible journalist. Who's that boy? He's an apprentice from the *Ideal*. I suppose they had no one else to send. So the apprentice goes back to being invisible. But he hears, he listens. He is informed by the low voices. Someone is talking about a scandal. In the corridors of the town hall, the Minister for Culture and Sport is annoyed with a theatre group. He lets it be known to an agent:

'How on earth could you decide to put on that play, the *Horrorsteia*.'

'It's not the *Horrorsteia*, it's the *Oresteia*.'

'Well, that just makes it worse!'

The theatre man cannot bear any more attacks from this cultural leader:

'The monster the rest of us carry inside, you have on the outside.'

The minister gazes down at the man from his position of authority. He needs an idea and waits for it to travel to his head. He is offended. It seems as if he is going to exact the most terrible vengeance. In the end, he says:

'Let's not start dropping hints, shall we?'

I internalised being an apprentice a great deal. As I did the fact of having gone into journalism as a result of a few poems. I managed to go to Madrid to study at the new faculty of Media

Studies. I was awarded a grant and sent almost daily chronicles for a section called 'North Station'. This is where we arrived on the Atlantic Express, eleven or twelve hours by train from A Coruña to Madrid. That bit about the poems is a stigma that forms part of my body. The first exercise we were given in the faculty had to do with journalistic language and precision. A subject that was close to my heart, as a gobbler of words. When the teacher, Federico Ysart, handed back our assignments, he threw mine on the table and said out loud, in a critical tone:

'This isn't journalism, it's literature!'

He was a very good professional, one of the best in that faculty, which had some really terrible teachers. He worked for an influential magazine, the weekly *Cambio 16*. But I recall with a certain pride that his verdict didn't hurt me. I felt content that my journalism should strike him as literature.

I was always an apprentice. I never stopped being one. I found this out on the day I interviewed a normal person.

I was doing work experience at the broadcasting centre of Spanish television in Galicia. The director was Alexandre Cribeiro, a poet as well as a producer. He'd worked for a long time in Madrid, where he'd been active in the UNESCO Club. It was summer. Santiago de Compostela. The permanent staff had gone on holiday. Cribeiro gathered us interns together and asked us something really rather unusual:

'What television would you like to make?'

We had ideas, but they slipped through our fingers. They weren't used to taking possession.

'The BBC!' said a whisper.

'Well, go ahead then!' said Cribeiro ironically. 'No, really. What topic should we cover first?'

There was a lot of controversy at the time about the first law to deal with the voluntary termination of pregnancy. The so-called abortion law. Up until then, women could go to prison if they aborted. During that period of transition, debate wasn't possible. Only the burning of words and anathemas.

'Don't even think about abortion,' said Cribeiro, divining our thoughts.

Yes, if we were the BBC, abortion would be the number one item on the agenda.

Cribeiro accepted with one condition:

'You have to begin the bulletin with three opinions, each with the same margin of time. A representative of the Church who is against the law. A woman in favour. And then a man or a woman, the opinion of a normal person.'

That seemed simple enough. Especially in Santiago. The cameraman and I emerged onto Obradoiro Square and soon got a statement from Canon Precedo. It wasn't difficult locating a feminist voice either. In Santiago, these two souls – the reactionary and the liberal – have lived side by side for ages, like the scallop shell that can be a symbol of Mars or Venus. All we needed now was the 'normal person'.

At the time, we still worked with celluloid. Connected by the microphone cable, the cameraman and I constituted a hybrid species of futuristic archaeology, moving slowly but eagerly. The cameraman knew the city better than me. I asked him:

'How about that one there?'

'That one? He's more stubborn than a mule.'

'What about that one over there?'

'He could eat the stones of the cathedral!'

An hour and a half later, with the deadline for going back to the studio drawing closer, I realised how difficult it can be to find a normal person when you need one.

154

We were about to give up when I saw her.

We were in the middle of Toural Square, next to the fountain, and she entered through the side. As soon as she came in, she saw us. And we saw her. The cameraman looked at me. And nodded. This was the one. She was carrying bags in both her hands, which hindered her movements. We cut her off diagonally. She tried to escape down an alley, but the cable enabled us to perform an enveloping manoeuvre that prevented her from leaving the arches.

There she was, opposite me. Panting in amazement. A normal person.

'Madam,' I asked straight away, 'what is your opinion about the law for the termination of pregnancy, the so-called abortion law?'

I was afraid she might scream. Cry out for help. But she calmed down and fixed me with a stare:

'Listen, boy. I'm not from around here, I just came to buy some shoes.'

We raced to the studio to open the news. She was the one. We had her at last. A normal person.

22

The Anarchist Woman's Smile

It was a beautiful Sunday. María had asked me to go with her to a coastal town where there was going to be a painting competition out in the open. On the coach, she sat next to the window. Everything outside produced light. She also had a little something for that Sunday light. The ferment of colours in her cloth-lined wicker basket, which contained brushes, oils, jars, and the porcelain bowls she used for mixing. The participants had to choose a section of the local landscape. I remember María painted some seaside houses, one of which had a tavern on the ground floor. It was an architecture in retreat, but which re-emerged that day with the light, the desire for style of naval colours, the tavern door like a songful, mysterious mouth. I wandered about, observing and comparing. My eyes didn't lie, couldn't lie. In María's painting, the reconstruction of the memory of colours, there was something I couldn't find anywhere else. When it came time to announce the winners, in the evening, in the town hall, María's painting was awarded the prize of honour.

Our return was silent and bitter. In theory, this prize of honour was the top award. But the ones that paid money were the other awards, which went to local painters. On top of that, the recipient of the prize of honour was obliged to donate their painting to the organisers. So we headed home with the sense of having been honourably done over. María with her basket of colours and painful smile. I think this was a mark of the house. My father gave voice to destiny, as if the stones already knew: 'The devil lurks behind the cross!'

For María, it was always important to earn a living by her own means. From when she was young, she gave classes in summer to small children in Castro. From a young age, while studying for her baccalaureate, she formed part of the resistance to Franco. She was active, very involved, with left-wing clandestine groups such as Red Flag. One Sunday, my mother woke me up in a fluster. She had opened a trapdoor in the henhouse and come across a pile of pamphlets. I lied. Said, 'They're mine.' This calmed her down. She was always more afraid for María. She had the feeling María was ahead of her time. And she was right. María distanced herself from Marxist groups, but not from the fight, when she understood that the idea of changing the world should go hand in hand with a new of life. She lived life as an anarchist. She left to study philology in Santiago, always in search of work to keep herself going. Nothing was beneath her. She was a great fan of arts and crafts. She made her own clothes, her own furniture. She fixed any problems in the places where she lived, with her box of melancholic tools, which all looked like unique specimens, the survivors of old workshops. She would go out foraging in orchards and by the sea. She was a gleaner of the kind painted by Millet, always searching for something useful in what had been hidden or abandoned. There were shop windows in front of which she would always stop to gaze: bookshops and ironmongeries. Groceries as well, where she would gather boxes to make bookshelves for her library. In her library, grammars sat alongside a DIY manual, and *The Book of Good Love* by the Archpriest of Hita rubbed shoulders with a book she held in high esteem: *Anarchist Aesthetics* by André Reszler. She recycled everything. In her ideas, she devised her own garden, her own company, with people like Kropotkin, Henry David Thoreau, Herman Hesse, and the texts of the Situationist International and the movement Provo ('provoke'), impelled by the Kabouters (anarchist 'gnomes'). She fed like the woodcock, the wood's guardian: she became vegetarian. She used to joke, 'Anarchist? Have you any idea how difficult that is!'

Her other passion was words. The deambulation of words. Their metamorphoses. Their ways of re-existing. She went after them, as she used to go looking for lucky ladybirds or glow-worms in the nocturnal walls of Castro as a child. She carried words in her pockets. On bits of paper scattered about the house like autumn leaves. In notebooks she herself had bound. And, if she had nothing else, then the palms of her hands, her arms, her

María Rivas

skin would act as parchment. When she was out of work, she did translations from English and French for the dubbing of films. A job she shared with Lois Pereiro. Sometimes, the two of them would laugh out loud when working on the dubbing of a porno film. 'Mm, mm, like that, like that, mm, mm, yes, yes, no, yes, I'm coming, not coming, coming, yes, yes, yes!' The technique involved turning moans into words. Because they were paid by the word, including monosyllables (I think now, with impatient capitalism, they only pay for words with a stress on the antepenultimate syllable). It was occasional work that didn't last long. Where she worked for longer, with the devotion of a gleaner of words, was on the team that compiled the Galician Academy's dictionary.

We coincided for a time in Santiago. I was studying and working in Madrid, but returned to Galicia to join the team of the weekly magazine *Teima*, the first to be published in Galician after the Second Republic. It was a time of great upheaval, great disappointments and hopes, during which the regime endeavoured to outlive the dictator, and the ground of history seemed as fragile as a thin layer of ice. Some say it was a failure, that weekly magazine, together with others like it that sprouted up all over Spain. What strikes me as miraculous is that the spring for us should last a whole year. Carrying out reports, in a single day, you underwent the sensation in one place of being received as a saviour of words and in another, not far away, of enduring the gears of silence-piercing hatred. María went with me to some of the more risky locations. She was there on the day of As Encrobas, 15 February 1977, when dozens of guards surrounded the area in order to expropriate lands that were earmarked for mining. Peasant women on the front line, resisting rifle blows with their umbrellas. All day, until sunset. María couldn't bear it. She didn't want to be a witness only. She forgot all about me.

She went over to the women to attend to their wounds. On her knees, in the mud, covered in dirt and blood. The guards, panting heavily, furious about the outcome, some uneasy, passed in front of the kneeling girl, her bright white skin smeared with dirt, as if they couldn't see her. At nightfall, she got up and returned without a word to where the photographer and I were standing.

Chagall talked about the coloured horses Russian workers and peasants painted at his art school to adorn the streets during the first May Day parade to be celebrated after the revolution. After that, there weren't any more horses, only official portraits. Our coloured horses were those experiences of indomitable journalism in the Spain of the transition, rebelling against the fatality of things being 'tied and well tied'. We would end up enduring the grey 'restoration'.

For a time, María and I shared an old apartment in Algalia, a district of Santiago. It had dripping water in every room (the Weatherman's stick again!) and the odd mystery. One day, we heard whispers in the attic. There was a door that was always closed. Until we decided to open it any way we could. There was a little man, a simpleton, who had been locked away. He spent the days eating sunflower seeds. The whole floor was covered in husks. He didn't speak. He only expressed himself with onomato-poeias. He didn't move. The look of surprise when he saw an unknown girl and boy opening the door. He traced a smile. The smile of pain. He had a nice face that made him look younger than he really was. We spoke to the landlady. She said we weren't to give it any importance. He was timid enough. Yes, but what was he doing locked up in the attic? The following day, when we woke up, he wasn't there anymore. There were traces of sunflower seeds on the stairs.

María was the only one in our family to know that I had been arrested in Madrid. A concealment to prevent family concern. I had arrived in September 1974. I would turn seventeen in October. It was more or less around my birthday. At a demonstration, at nightfall, on Princesa Street. The police had been tipped off. Our initial shouts were a signal for them to charge. They emerged from every direction. A real ambush. A group of demonstrators ran up a dead-end street like lambs following the orders of the boldest among us, who bore a certain resemblance to the poet Leopoldo María Panero. A comic episode, had we not ended up in the most feared building in Madrid at that time – the national police headquarters on the Puerta del Sol. There were so many of us in the dead-end street they took us there by bus. Most of us were detained for two days in cells packed with people, after we had identified ourselves, stripped down and had our photographs taken. Five people had been squeezed into my cell, but nobody felt much like talking. I was led upstairs to an office to be questioned. It wasn't a historic moment. Of the two officers present, one didn't even look at me, taken up as he was with intellectual labours. The other asked me to identify myself again. 'So you're Galician? Your accent gives you away.' As always when it came to the question of phonetics, I was reminded of César Vallejo – 'The accent dangles from my shoe' – but this time I didn't want to bring poems into it.

'Yes.'

'And are you on the other side? Against Franco?'

'Yes.'

He gave me a very professional slap across the face and reminded me that Franco was also Galician.

'So you're the one who's stupid.'

I didn't reply to this. I was struggling to establish a connection between my accent and being opposed to Franco or not. I felt uneasy that the other policeman, the intellectual, might include the term 'nitwit' in my record to describe my affiliation. In my nightmare, I was hopeful he would at least write 'useful nitwit'. That was about it. They had too much work that day to be wasting their time with a snotty student. One of my cellmates, a young worker, came back from questioning with a broken nail and a bloody hand. Not a word of complaint. He didn't even allow them a gesture of pain. He deserved the company of someone like Max Estrella in *Bohemian Lights*, but we all stayed quiet, perhaps in the absurd hope that the murmurs and footsteps coming from the pavements of the Puerta del Sol were the echoes of liberating hordes. Nothing. All the echoes vanished into the night. I didn't feel like a fighter. I was – we were – humiliated people. The following day, a man turned up with a bucket of lentils. He gave us each a zinc bowl and poured in a spoonful of slops. From time to time, he would say, 'Shit!' And let out a laugh.

Boh.

When they hurt, María and I would share our secrets.

Her skin was very white and had freckles the colour of maize bread. I liked her way of being. Her body as well. Her virtually transparent skin. The hydrography of her veins. Her cereal freckles. One day, in Algalia, we embraced as a result of the groundswells. She was crying because of a lost love. I was down in the dumps because of some other disenchantment. We fell asleep in that bed so well suited to shipwrecks: surrounded by buckets and bowls to collect the dripping water.

But this time it didn't knock.

The news of her illness arrived when I was in Ireland with

Isabel and the children. Isabel was one of the five girls who lived above the bar Dos Ciudades. We were now staying north of the Liffey river, in Temple Villas, right next to the prison on Arbour Hill, which helped keep the rent down. We felt comfortable, at ease, in that Dublin where on a Saturday, near the house, in Smithfield, there would be a horse and potato market. Nobody had come up with the term 'Celtic Tiger' yet. In some pubs, they still remembered O'Brien, the man who always kept his right hand in a glove because he'd promised his mother, on her deathbed, that he would never touch a glass of alcohol again. The women selling products in large prams on Moore Street would say to whoever fondled the tomatoes, 'They're not pricks, love! The more you squeeze them, the softer they get.'

It was my sister Chavela who called. There were no mobiles, but the ring of the landline was clear enough. Now I knew why my father never lifted the receiver. He could scent the approach of destiny. María was sick. How sick? Very sick. They're going to operate on her, but it would seem she has metastasis. She did. It was already too late. One day, I went with her to Santiago. She wanted to speak to the doctor who had operated on her the first time. There was no hope, either in the words or in the eyes or in the gestures of this man. I looked around his consultation room. The walls were bare. Cast in shadow. The doctor spoke with half his face lit up by a desk lamp.

'I had to come back,' said María when we left. 'My own journey to the heart of darkness.'

In the room where María died, in Castro, both my father and my mother died in a relatively short space of time. On the eve of her death, my mother woke up with a strange sense of energy. After a series of long days in bed, she got up and changed the bedclothes; she wanted to do it herself, using white, luminous sheets of the kind she washed by hand. She then lay down and gave us one of her painful smiles. Farewell, farewell! When my father succumbed, he availed himself of all the coryphaeus' accumulated irony. He asked us to lift him in the orthopaedic bed, assembled by Paco, so he could climb up high and cure his vertigo once and for all. He then came out with a eulogy of mechanics: 'Industry has come a long way, thanks to us patients!'

Those of us who stayed behind had the impression they'd left like this, in a hurry, to go looking for their anarchist daughter. Yes, that was the room where María died. During the terminal phase of her illness, she had asked us to help her leave so she wouldn't have to suffer any more. Her hand reached out to help. The carnival giants, the Catholic Monarchs, were not in the window this time, rather the introverted green of the lemon tree that had grown in the coarse soil and rubble of the first house.

Acknowledgements

This book arose from a series of articles called 'Storyboard', published in the cultural supplement *Luces de Galicia* of the Galician edition of the newspaper *El País*. I would like to thank Xosé Hermida and Daniel Salgado for the kind attention and welcome they gave me. The articles then chose to ferment, and among the people who helped me to see into another time, to recollect, I am particularly grateful for the contributions of Manuel Bermúdez Chao and Carmelo Seoane, owner of A Artabria (Leonor's old shop and pub) in the Republic of Castro de Elviña. They were both also generous enough to provide photographs of the 'restless paradise'. Similarly generous was the photographer Xoán Piñón, who retrieved from his archives two photographs that show my sister María when she was young. Finally, my deepest gratitude goes to all my family and the company of low voices.